Miracles, Mysteries & Magic

Way Beyond the Sky, Where Dragons Rule, Volume 5

Jeri Andrew

Published by Jeri Andrew, 2023.

This is a work of fiction. Similarities to real people, places, or events are entirely coincidental.

MIRACLES, MYSTERIES & MAGIC

First edition. November 5, 2023.

Copyright © 2023 Jeri Andrew.

ISBN: 979-8223187509

Written by Jeri Andrew.

To Drew. There would be no series without you!

Volume 5
Miracles, Mysteries & Magic

1

Chapter 1

"Merrill, how's it going?" Healix asked the busy wizard.

"Well, I think I may be on to something here. Check out the vines growing from her blood."

"Those are growing from AlaHanDrea's blood?" Jax asked.

"Yes! Her blood contains the seeds of life! She told us to grow them, so, we did. I don't want to disturb those pods, but I sure am anxious to see what's in them!

In the mean time, I took some sap to analyze and I believe I have the chemicals needed for the antidote!"

"So, the antidote is actually coming from her, in a sense."

"Exactly!"

Healix spoke up, "I can't get over how much they've grown!"

"I know, right" Merrill agreed.

"Merrill, I'd like to apologize to you for misjudging you. I don't agree with who you follow, or, worship, not in the least, but I feel I've judged you to harshly,"

Jax told the seasoned wizard.

"So, truce?" Merrill asked.

"Ya, truce."

Braynar saw AlaHanDrea standing over by the fire. He walked up behind her and grabbed her bottom. She turned around and slapped him! "Hey, keep your hands to yourself! Yours is over there," she told him, pointing at the water falls.

"Well, excuse me! My bad, but hey, you look just like her!" He said in his own defense.

Danalli witnessed their exchange as he was walking up to camp, he learned from Braynar's mistake...

"So, which one of you gorgeous women belongs to me?" He said as he entered camp.

"Danalli! Hi baby!" She said as she went over and kissed Danalli hello.

Keithen walked into camp, "O.k. now, I know that one of you is mine, would the lucky woman please reveal herself to me?"

"Hi Keithen, I missed you today," she said as she walked over to give him a kiss.

"AlaHanDrea!" Chloe hollered as she walked up to camp. "Wow! Now I know how others feel when they see all of my sisters and me..."

"Chloe! So good to see you!"

"It's great to see you, too."

"AlaHanDrea, We all wanted you to be the first to know, seven of us are pregnant!"

"Really? Oh, how wonderful! I'm so excited for all y'all!"

"Thanks. We all love our lives and love you for giving us our lives. You're our hero, girl! And we all love you so much!"

"I love all y'all as well!"

"Well, I can't stay, I just wanted to stop by and share the news. Please get well soon, we need you here with us!" Chloe said, then kissed her cheek goodby.

AlaHanDreas and their men, all slipped off into their lairs for some good loving...

Leon came to claim his and shuffled off to go be alone with her.

———————

"Merrill, What you do is witchcraft. You have to understand, witchcraft goes against everything we believe in," Jax told him.

"Maybe so, but this witchcraft is what's going to save her life!"

"As it should, since witchcraft is what got her into this situation to begin with!" Jax commented, sarcastically.

"Now fellas, stop the bickering, now's not the time," Healix told them.

Healix went over to the plant and put his finger on one of the pods... Then made a viewing screen appear to show the contents...

It was a fetus!

"Well, I'll be! She can reproduce by herself! amazing!

The guys and their AlaHanDreas were all curled up together, enjoying the love they all just shared, when...

All of a sudden, the AlaHanDreas vanished!

Every one of them!

The guys were beside themselves!

In their hearts, they knew what it meant.

They all ran back up to the surface.

Leon ran back to camp to check with the others...

They summoned Isabel, yes, the ones with them vanished as well!

Isabel frantically sent a message to Healix!

"Oh no, I just got a message from Isabel! All of Baby Girls Copies just vanished!"

The panicked trio rushed to AlaHanDreas side. She was barely alive.

Merrill gave her the antidote, but nothing was helping.

A transparent AlaHanDrea stood before them...

"I love you guys! I've loved ever moment of my life that had you in it.

I will never forget you!

Please find out why my parents chose to end my life! I don't want to die, but the poison has destroyed my body. I will miss you all! Until we meet again, my friends!" She blew them a kiss.

"AlaHanDrea!

Please!

No!

Baby Girl, Don't go! Please baby girl, don't die!

Please don't die!" they all cried.

"It's not my first choice, I promise you that! Just know that I love you all!"

And she vanished.

"AlaHanDrea!

No!

No!

Baby girl!

No!

Come back sweet girl, oh please come back!" Jax screamed.

"Merrill, Healix, Do Something!"

____

Viewing screens popped up high in sky, all across the globe.

It is with a heavy heart that we come to you today.

On this day, the world has lost a beautiful soul.

A creature like no other...

Today, our beloved Queen AlaHanDrea has passed away at the tender age of 19. A creature meant to live for thousands of years has passed after only 19 short years...

She was poisoned by her own parents!

All attempts to revive her have failed.

She will be greatly and forever missed.

The world lost it's hero today.

May God have mercy on us all!"

Cries could be heard world wide for the death of the great Teen Queen, AlaHanDrea...

Celebration of life videos played around the clock on the huge screens suspended in air... Celebrating The Life and times of one of the most powerful creatures ever known.

Everyone was in utter disbelief that one such as her, was really gone.

Braynar, Keithen, Danalli, Kenneth, Leon, George and Isabel, Dane, Athena and King Neptune, Jax, Raynar, Barbara and too many others to name, fell into a deep grief for the unbelievable loss of someone they thought would outlive them all.

The world watched around the clock videos of the baby warrior, as she fought battles to defend a world of creatures she had never even met...

They watched videos of a 6 year old little girl leading a battalion of dragons into battle against aliens, then fighting for her own life afterwards.

They watched video after video of a beautiful girl child's selfless acts of bravery to defend the world they lived in and the whole world cried for her...

But none wept harder than those closest to her.

Grief gripped the animal kingdom.

A bounty was issued for her parents ...

Dead or alive...

Chapter 2

"Jax, the pods are growing pretty quickly. It looks as if they will be ready to open soon!

There are babies inside! We should call Isabel and Athena," Merrill told Jax.

"I agree. This is not a job for just the men!"

"Isabel! Athena! Please come at once!" Jax yelled out.

Both women were consumed with grief over AlaHanDrea's death, but they obeyed the summon.

"We called you here for a reason. When Merrill took a sample of AlaHanDrea's blood, he saw the seeds of life.

She told us to put them in soil and see what grew. So, we did.

These vines began to grow, then, these pods appeared.

Ladies, there are babies inside!

AlaHanDrea's babies!" Jax explained.

"Seriously? Wow! That's incredible!

Oh those poor babies! Their mommy is dead!" Isabel said.

"No, don't you see what's happening here? AlaHanDrea is about to be reborn!" Athena said.

"What?" Isabel asked.

"Look here, I'm a Goddess, I know about these things!"

"Athena, I don't mean to contradict you, but there are three, not one ," Healix commented.

"Maybe so, but I'm telling you, AlaHanDrea is Not Dead!" Athena insisted.

"Athena's not wrong," Mitchin told them.

"Mitchin! Dude, so good to see you!"

"Likewise.

Athena's not wrong! AlaHanDrea lives! She lives," Mitchin insisted. "Not only her spirit, but her.

Remember when we saw the light of God in her direction? Well, now, it can honestly be said that she is a gift from God Himself! She is about to be born all over again..."

The group looked at the pods, they were growing by the second...

"But, there are three of them!" Isabel said.

"OMG! 3 baby AlaHanDreas?" Jax said.

"What are their names?" Merrill asked.

Mitchin spoke up, "Aleha, Hannah and AlaHanDrea. We won't know which is which until they are born. AlaHanDrea herself, not a copy, but our baby girl is about to be reborn!"

Isabel stepped outside, as did Athena. Isabel summoned the guys and Athena summoned her father and Dane.

They all came right away.

The ladies filled them in on what was going on. Just as they finished, Merrill hollered for them to come quick! The pods were about to open!

Isabel called for the creature royalty, bears, wolves, big cats, unicorns, centaurs and especially the fairies.

A huge crowd was assembled, so a viewing screen was put up.

Everyone watched as the pods moved in every which direction, until one of them finally burst open enough for the fluid to come pouring out.

A moment later, the pod fell away to reveal the most beautiful baby girl, sitting up, rubbing her eyes. When she opened them, she began laughing, clapping her tiny hands and bounced on her butt....

Cheers could be heard from outside as everyone looked on....

Braynar, Keithen, Danalli, Kenneth and Leon pushed their way inside.

"Wow! She's so beautiful!" Leon said. The baby looked at him and reach out for him to come pick her up.

Athena was busy washing her off, so Leon had to wait, making her fuss, so, Leon took over the task of cleaning her up. It excited her, making her laugh and coo...

The second pod began tearing open.

Moments later, another baby girl was revealed, only she was tiny in comparison and was more like a newborn human infant. Isabel picked her up and began cleaning her up.

The third pod had a tiny hole pierce, allowing the fluid to slowly leak out.

The baby Inside, tore a small hole with her fingers, to peek out of... Then, ever so slowly, the pod finished ripping open.

She looked identical to the other two, and like the first one, seemed to have good motor skills as well as awareness...

She saw Braynar and reached for him to take her.

His heart melted... Who could say no to that? He picked her up and helped finish cleaning her up.

"Hi there, precious girl, is your name Aleha?" Braynar asked the baby.

She looked at him with a blank look on her face.

Danalli stepped over and reached for the baby Braynar was holding. She smiled a big smile and reached for him.

Braynar handed her to Danalli. "Oh,, what a precious little one! Waiting for you to grow up is going to be so hard! Yes it is! But we are all here to help you do it," Danalli told her.

Keithen reached out for her. She turned her head.

"Well," he said, teasingly.

She turned her head back towards him, gave him a naughty smile, then reached for him.

Danalli just laughed and handed her over to him.

The baby Leon was holding reached for Kenneth. He smiled real big and nervously took her in his arms. "She's so precious! Welcome to the world, little one."

She smiled big and blew spit bubbles.

"So, Mitchin, which one is AlaHanDrea and are the others her too? Or, are they her children? What's the deal?" Healix asked.

I believe the first baby is AlaHanDrea reborn. The world has grieved long enough. It's time to make the announcement," Mitchin said.

"I AwaHawDweeea." The baby Danalli was holding, said.

Everyone looked in astonishment! She spoke! She was also growing rather rapidly. She was already the size of of a 6 month old and growing.

Athena began crying! Dane finally came into the room. The baby looked at Dane and started to hold her arms out, then said, "Dane," then put her arms down and had a tear running down her cheek.

Dane turned and walked back out of the room.

King Neptune looked at his son questioningly...

"That baby looks exactly like AlaHanDrea did as a baby."

"Son, that Is AlaHanDrea, reborn."

"AlaHanDrea is dead, daddy."

"Dane, she lives again! That's her, not a copy or offspring, it's her, in a brand new body!"

"How's that even possible, daddy?"

"All things are possible with God, son. She found favor with Him. He showed her Mercy."

"What about her memories, Daddy?"

"It looked to me as tho her memories are in tact, or, at least partially in tact."

"SO, NOW WHAT? WHO IS going to take care of these babies?" Merrill asked.

Barbara stepped up and said, "Me. I will help, with the tiniest one, especially."

"Do you have any idea how dangerous these babies are?" Jax asked her.

"It's a tiny baby!" Barbara argued.

"It's a tiny baby that may absorb you or even turn you to vapor and inhale you." Jax insisted.

"Oh, well then, who else? I'm just going to trust AlaHanDrea to remember who I am and not to hurt me.. anyway, her and I are connected, she's part of me! No, I trust her and I will help take care of her."

"I will help take care of her," Celia volunteered. "I nursed her the first time she was a baby and I can do it again. I have milk."

"Of course I will help watch over them," Athena said.

The sound of rhythm drums signaled the fairies marching in. "Well, I guess that answers the question, doesn't it?" Merrill said. When they turned and looked, the first baby, AlaHanDrea, had grown significantly! She was the size of a toddler and was standing up! The other babies remained the same.

"Wow! Well, that answers another question, which one is AlaHanDrea!" Jax said.

"I Quee AwahawDweeeeea!!!!! ". The toddler shouted!

"Well, yes you are! Welcome back, baby girl!" Braynar said.

"I back!"

"Her growth compared to the others growth, answers another question. The other 2 are offspring," Healix told them.

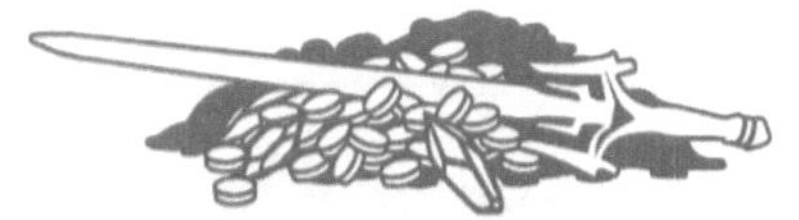

Chapter 3

Braynar stood up, "I'll watch over her tonight. Danalli and Keithen can take the next 2 shifts. Franklon and Brian can stand guard first and Keithen and Danalli can choose their own guards."

"I don't think 2 guards are enough," Isabel told them "I don't believe for one second that her parents acted alone! Pardon me for saying so, but they don't strike me as being bright enough to even know about the poison."

"I don't know about that, Folica killed herself with poison," Keithen said.

"Still, I think someone convinced them to kill her!" Isabel insisted.

"I still can't believe they did it. I mean, I know they did, I just can't believe they killed their own child!" Danalli said. "I'm prone to agree with Isabel.

"Boys, she lives. As do her offspring. She provided herself a new body to live in, exactly like the old one. Or, as far as we know, like the old one. She's reborn," Isabel said again.

"This is all so hard to grasp," Kenneth added.

"O.k. Braynar gets first watch. She's growing very quickly. Ask for volunteers from the big cats, wolves and bears for additional guard, don't leave them out. I'm going to go talk to Bjorn and King Leon about assistance in investigating the murder." Isabel told them. "Take good care of her, Braynar."

"Yes, mother."

When Isabel stepped out, a slew of female dragons, Tootsie and Cathey Ann leading the pack, stood ready to assist. Isabel felt much better with the girls there.

"Has it occurred to anyone else that AlaHanDrea is an extremely powerful and dangerous creature, alien creature, that has managed to get the whole world at her beck and call? I mean, let's play what if, for a moment. What if this whole thing is a set up?

What if she poisoned herself, knowing that she'd have a new body? She's very angry at her parents, what better way to get rid of them without the blame being on her? The only proof we have that her parents are involved, is her word... What if it's all an elaborate scheme?" Merrill suggested. "

I mean, she has the royalty of the watchers as well as dragon kind, big cats, wolves, bears, etc .. bowing at her pretty little feet!"

"Merrill, I hear what you're saying, but she already had us all bowing at her pretty little feet!" George responded.

"Ya, we'd already die for her," Jax added.

"We ALL, including you, owe that child our lives! She has saved the inhabitants of this planet more grief than you realize. She is nothing short of Amazing.

Everyone has a dark side, including AlaHanDrea, but we've yet to see it. Well, o.k., so we got a peek when she was absorbing my brother, but she was still very young..." Healix said.

"So, it's your belief that her parents really did poison her," Merrill asked.

"They poisoned her and Tommy! She knocked the drink from Tommy's hand before he could drink it, then she passed out. Anyone else would have died on the spot," Raynar told him.

"What do you think their motive was?" Merrill asked.

"Personally, I think they were talked into it. I think someone convinced them to kill her. That way, her parent would take the blame, eliminating the probability of them making another baby," George explained.

"Well, ya, that does make sense. So, summon her parents. Summon them to where they must obey!" Merrill told them.

"Merrill, if you can do that, have at! There is a bounty on their heads. Go for it!" George replied.

"Excuse me majesties, AlaHanDrea's parents are here to turn themselves in!" Brian showed the couple in. They were inside of a forcefield bubble, clutching each other, scared out of their wits!

"Sit! You don't need that bubble in here. Take it down or be destroyed," George ordered.

They obeyed.

Both of them were staring at the floor.

"Just tell us why you murdered AlaHanDrea! Why did you do it!" George demanded.

"Because it was our duty to do so! We made her, it was up to us to kill her," Jefry explained.

"But, why?" Jax asked.

"Several reasons.

I love Folica very much. We got off to a very rough start.

Things were not supposed to happen the way they did!

Everything got all messed up!

Once we saw each other again, we realized just how much we really do love one another.

We have been in love from the moment we set eyes on each other.

Folica should not have had to go through all of that alone.

Had we been together still, we could have killed the monster child together, when she was born!

As it should have been! But, instead, Folica killed herself, not the child!

It should have been the child that died that day, not Folica!" Jefry explained.

"What? Wait, what? Why did the child need to die at all? She saved Folica! Folica would not be here today were it not for that child!" George snapped, anger building from deep within.

"That child is a Monster! A very powerful monster! She MUST be destroyed!" Jefry told him.

"That child is your Daughter!" George snapped.

"Exactly! And it's our responsibility to make sure she is destroyed!" He insisted.

"Why Tommy? Why did you try to poison Prince Tommy?" Jax asked him.

"Because we were offered a reward large enough to sustain us in the humans world for the rest of our lives, if we would kill him," Jefry told him.

"Who offered you a reward to kill Tommy?" Jax asked him.

"The resistance. General Peabody of the human resistance. He offered us a bounty to kill them both.

They are a good and strong group," Jefry explained.

"Jefry, they offered you enough to sustain you for the rest of your lives, because if we don't kill you, they will.

They see you as an abomination and want you just as dead as they want your child!

You made AlaHanDrea! Do you actually think they would allow you to live and risk you reproducing again?" George asked him.

"Oh." Was all Jefry said. Folica said not a word.

"I don't understand your desire to kill your own child, I just don't get it! She may be a monster, but have you looked in a mirror lately, Jefry? You, sir, are the very definition of a monster!

We all are, for that matter! The world is full of monsters!

We are all learning to cohabitate in peace, but monsters we still are!" Jax explained.

"Well, that very well may be true, but Folica and I want to start over and how can we do that if AlaHanDrea were to live? She is part of our past! We want to wipe the slate clean and begin again... It's all a mute point now, anyway, the child is dead already." Jefry said.

"Jefry, you murdered the most incredible creature this world has ever known!

You murdered her!

How do you expect to continue to live?

Don't you realize you bought a death sentence?

The penalty for murder is death!" George scolded.

"You mean, you're going to kill us? You can't do that!" Jefry said in a panic.

"Sure we can and yes, Jefry, we are going to kill you both! You murdered AlaHanDrea! You WILL be put to death!"

"But you can't do that!"

"And just why not?"

"Well, because this is us! Jefry and Folica and we are starting over! It's not fair!"

"Not fair?" You speak of fair?

You MURDERED AlaHanDrea!" George yelled.

"Right!

We are her parents!

We Made Her!

Folica and I Made Her!

It's within our rights to end what we began!"

"No! It is NOT!" George argued.

"YES, IT IS! She belongs to Us!

Not you!

We Made Her!

She's Ours!

If we choose to end her, that's our decision to make, not yours!

Our child, our choice!

Beasts kill their own children all the time!

Some beasts eat their own children!

Can you stand there and deny that?

So what you're telling me, even though you're beasts, you're now living by humanities rules?"

"Guards, lock them in Chambers, together. Now, before I kill them myself!

Ready the troops, it's time for a fly.... Time to visit the resistance!

Send king Leon in here at once! And king Bjorn, King William, send them all in, at once! Go, Now!" George commanded.

"Yes, George, you wanted to see us?" King Leon Asked.

"Yes, I'm asking that all of you here before me today, are now, and hereafter, formally a part of the counsel of Kings.

What say you?" George asked.

"Here here!" They all said in Unison.

Communication screens went up, the entire counsel of Kings were present.

George explained everything Jefry had told them about the human resistance.

The counsel called the human president, to fill him in on the state of affairs and let him know what was about to happen on his continent.

They let him know that the counsel now included kings of ALL species! Man kind was vastly out numbered!

"Squash the resistance! Or burn!!!" George demanded.

"Your resistance is responsible for the death of AlaHanDrea and the attempted murder of Prince Tommy!

They will be turned over to Dragon kind immediately, or we will begin to burn your continent, do you understand me?

Am I making myself perfectly clear?

Do you need it further explain to you?

You have 24 hours to produce the resistance leaders!

General Peabody in particular!

We want the ones responsible for the murder and attempted murder of a Queen and a Wolf Prince of the beast communities and we want them now!

They will be executed publicly for the world to see!

Produce them, or burn!

So says I, so says this counsel! All in favor?" George asked.

A collective "I" was said... it was unanimous!

"George, you and I have known each other for a very long time.

Please, I beg of you, give me a chance to bring the guilty parties forward.

Please I beg of you, do not fly!

Please, do not fly!

So many Innocents will die!

I beg of you, do not burn our cities, do not burn our villages!

The resistance does not represent humanity!

They do not.

George, I see that you have included the royalty of the other species in the council and I respectfully request that I be added to the counsel of Kings... I am a president, not a king, but I'm still leader of humanity, a species of mammals and I ask that I be added to the council of Kings for the planet.

Fair is fair, after all,

George. And George, I've always known you to be fair!

I swear to you, the resistance does not represent humanity!

These rebels will be dealt with!

I assure you, we will bring them to you and deliver them to your feet... just please, I beg of you, don't punish all of humanity for the crimes of these few!

We're so sorry for what they have done!

Our hearts are broken for the loss of such a beautiful queen!

George, we all loved her too!

Everyone fell in love with that beautiful creature!

We watched her grow up and blossom into a woman... We watched a small girl child defend our world! We love her too and I beg of you George! Please! We are on your side! We laughed when she laughed, cried when she cried... We watched young love blossom...

We cannot believe that she has been murdered!

We grieve with you over her loss and are appalled that humans are responsible, either in whole or in part.

But I beg of you, George, please let us join you to help make this right... Well, there's no making it right... she's gone... but please, help us bring Justice to this senseless murder," Carl pleaded.

"Carl, you make some very valid points. Your request to be included in the council of Kings is granted.

You're right, fair is only fair.

You're one of the world's leaders, therefore you should sit on the council.

I hear you Carl.

I hear you well.

Okay, but you still have 24 hours. If you can't produce the resistance in 24 hours, that's not our problem, it's yours.

I suggest you do a broadcast and allow your citizens to save themselves, by turning over the culprits and we don't want people sacrificed, declared the leaders!

We're not stupid!

We want the true leaders and we know when you're lying and you know we do!

We have watchers sitting on our council and an angel! We Know when you're lying!"

"George, with the counsels permission, I will broadcast our conversation in its entirety to all of Humanity at once."

"Thank you, Carl. And Carl, please switch over to a private channel..."

"O.k. I'm here, what's up?"

"Carl, when the wizard, Merrill, drew some of AlaHanDrea's blood, he saw the seeds of life. She insisted they be planted in soil. Vines began to grow and before long, pods formed. Inside the pods were babies, Carl!

3 babies!

1 of which, is AlaHanDrea, reborn!

The other 2 are her offspring!

Carl, she lives again! She's still a baby, but is growing very quickly...

We are more than amazed at this phenomenon!

None of us have ever seen anything like this before, it's incredible!

We all stood here and witnessed their birth, it occurred a few hours ago.

Carl, she lives on!!!"

"Praise be!

Oh George!

Praise be! " Carl was honestly excited to hear the news.

"Keep this silent for now.

Tell no one, or we fly!

She's been returned to us!

The world will know once the resistance is dealt with." George commanded.

"Understood!" Carl agreed.

Chapter 4

"Dad, please bring the humans to feed the baby. She needs to absorb a few and consume a few, before she's offered a breast, or she may end up absorbing the creature with the breast. These ladies need to be able to safely nurse her," Braynar told George.

"Danalli went and got them, son."

"Thanks, dad."

"Bwaynars... Bwwaynars...

Bwwwaynars...

Teeheeheehee,"

"Baby girl, your so pretty, yes you are! Such a sweet baby! Yes you are! I didn't get to see you as an infant before... What a precious baby you are!"

"Wubs my Bwaynarse..."

"I love you too, baby girl! Thank you for coming back to me!

My heart was shattered...

I didn't know how I was going to live without you! I couldn't even breath!

This Is you, isn't it?"

The baby girl wrapped her hand around Braynar's finger... Images of their time spent together ran through his head. She looked deep into his eye, " is me, Bwaynarse, me baby gin."

"Yes, you're a baby again and I still love you!"

"I ... Pwomis uh gwo up fass I can..."

"I know you will sweet girl! I know you will."

"Hugwy... Hugwy... I hugwy... Boohoohoohoo awah... Huh, uh wahhhahaha...

"Now, now, AlaHanDrea, stop that, now come on, foods coming..."

"Bwahahahaha!!!!"

"Dad! Hurry! Please! Hurry!" Braynar pleaded.

Braynar sent telepathic messages to his brothers, "it's her, it's our AlaHanDrea. She looked me right in the eye and said, is me... Then, she wrapped her little hand around my finger and showed me images of us together. It really is her. It's her, guys. It's her... And she's pitching a fit because she's hungry!"

"Bro, I got here as fast as I could!" Danalli said, as he pulled the food wagon in.

"Wahahahaha bawhahahaha uhwahhhahaha!"

"I see the broadcast drone is following you around now."

"Oh, that, ya, well, everything AlaHanDrea is huge news right now, including this little hungry fit! Listen to you, baby girl!" Danalli replied.

"Bwahahahahahahahaaaa uhwahahahahaaa!"

"Ya, I suppose it is. Hey, General, why are you looking so scared? Relax dude. You know, I completely understand where you're coming from, dude. How would you like to get out of that cage and I don't know, hold the baby for a minute? I mean, you do like kids, don't you? I mean you don't have to. But she's kind of fussy and I need to get her food ready, so if you don't mind, I mean, I'll let you out of the cage." Braynar told him.

"Well, ya, o.k. actually, I thought you brought me here to kill me."

"Kill you? Me? Na, not my thing tonight."

The general reluctantly stepped out of the cage, walked over & took the baby. He held her in his arms, then sat down with her. She stopped crying when he took her.

"Wow, I think the baby likes me. She settled right down."

"Ya, she sure seems to like you. So, tell me General, what exactly is this resistance. What are y'all resisting?"

"Excuse me your highnesses, I don't mean to disturb you, but, the ladies are here to feed the baby Queen," Brian told them.

"Highnesses? Baby Queen?" The general asked.

"Yes,, allow me to introduce us, I'm Crowned Prince Braynar and this is Crowned Prince Danalli, heirs to the throne of Drakonia.

That was my girlfriend you had murdered."

The general got a whole new sense of terror....

He suddenly realized that he was no longer holding the baby! He looked around, but didn't see her... All of a sudden he began to convulse! Moments later, he was gone and a much larger baby sat smiling where he once sat, cooing and gooing... Smiling and blowing spit bubbles.

"Mo pweese..." Then she burped and said "Scuse me!" Then giggled.

The other humans in the cage sat terrified!

"So, who wants to hold the baby next?" Danalli asked the other humans.

"What, no volunteers? Ah c'mon, she's such a pretty little thing..."

AlaHanDrea turned 2 of the men to vapor and inhaled them, burped and said, "Scuse me," again, then giggled.

She held her little hand out in front of her, opening and closing her little fists. One of the men began sliding across the cage towards her. He slammed up against the bars. She kept opening and closing her little fists... The man screamed as he pushed against the bars... She pulled her hands towards her body while opening and closing her fists... The mans body began breaking as he was pulled through the bars, then she moved her hands up and down and the man bounced off of the floor until he was dead and all busted up. "Bad Man's! Bad Man's wit poisoms, bad man gibs mommy poisoms kiws me... Me kiws bad mans!!!!! Bad Man's!!! Nudder bad mans! Nudder one n nudder ones too! Bad Man's

kiws me ded! Bad Man's! Now I kiws u! Bad Man's....." She hollered...
Bwaynarse kiws de badman's! Pweeze..."

"You want me to kill the next one, baby girl?"

"Uh huh, eat dem swowy..."

"Sure. I am kinda hungry, now that you mention it. Do you want
Danalli's to eat one too?"

"Uh h huh ya I do!"

"Danalli, shall we?"

"So, these are the men that gave your parents the poison to kill
you?" Danalli asked her.

"Yep... Das dem!"

"Ya, I could eat. Shall we, bro?"

"Weeew swow... "

"Ok baby girl, anything for you!"

"You ass holes see that baby right there? That's the woman you
murdered. She's been reborn and it's time for you to pay for her death!"

"Me bite pweeze"?

"Sure baby girl, you can have a bite, too," Both of the guys told her.

5 men remained in the cage, watching, while Braynar and Danalli
shifted to dragon state and began very slowly eating the other 2.

"Once they had finished their meal, they terrorized the remaining
men, before shifting back to their gorgeous human looking selves.

"Oh stop shaking, ya big cry babies. Y'all get to live... Until the next
feeding time, anyway... "

Braynar used his magic to cover the cage.

AlaHanDrea was sitting on the ground on her blanket, playing
with her fingers and toes, then tipped over on her back and put her toes
in her mouth. Danalli and Braynar couldn't help but to laugh at how
precious she was as an infant.

"These are special moments, bro!" Danalli said.

"Yes, they really are," Braynar agreed.

"Look at how big she is since she had her meal!" Braynar exclaimed.

"Excuse me, boys, is it safe for me to feed her yet?" Cecilia asked.

"Sure, come on in. AlaHanDrea, look whose here! She has breast milk for you! Yummy bear milk! Now AlaHanDrea, never, ever absorb the women who nurse you!" Danalli told her.

"I goo girws"

"I know you're a good girl, baby. Enjoy your milk."

"You boys worry too much! Come here sweet girl! Here, how about I lay down with you and you can drink from any one you want to drink from! You can even drink from all of them if you like. Do you know how to nurse?" Cecilia asked her as she squirted milk into the babies mouth.

AlaHanDrea wasted no time emptying all of Cecilia's breasts! Afterwards, she burped and fell asleep.

"Kareena is feeding the other two," Cecilia told the guys. " They are not growing nearly as fast as this one is. The tiny one doesn't seem to be very strong. She isn't responding to being fed. We may have to force feed her. The poor little thing doesn't look... Well, you boys know what I mean."

"Oh, that's sad to hear." Braynar said. " Do they know why?"

"No. Some babies just don't... ... ... "

"Right."

" Isabel and Athena have her. King Neptune is doing all he can and Dane is helping, too. Danes wife has asked to adopt her."

"Oh wow! Is George going to allow it?" Danalli asked.

"He's not going to stop it."

"What about the whole under water thing?"

"She wants to use part of the resort,"

"Oh, good idea," Braynar commented.

"Danes wife actually loves AlaHanDrea and always has. She has no problem at all with Dane being with her. More then anything, she wants a chance to focus on caring for the tiny newborn. She wants to save the tiny girl. She's AlaHanDrea's daughter and AlaHanDrea is in no condition to take care of the infant herself.

She asked for the other child, Aleha, but, Isabel and Athena both said no.

Aleha is amazing, guys! She's obviously the daughter of this one!

She is SO much like her mother!

But, she's not growing nearly as quickly.

This one looks like she's trying to become an adult over night!"

"Aleha is healthy then?" Danalli asked.

"Healthy, alert, magical, hungry and demanding! She also keeps asking for her mommy. Is there a reason we have them separated?" Cecilia asked.

"Fear," Braynar answered. "Pure fear! So much power in the hands of infants is terrifying! We are trying to avoid accidents."

"Oh, well, right. That makes sense, but, they are magical. If you don't voluntarily allow them to be together, they make take it upon themselves... Then, you won't have any control at all. It would be a huge mistake to allow them to take control," Cecilia warned.

"Wow, I hadn't thought about that. Maybe Dane and Dana ought to bring Hanna and stay close by as well. Ya, we need to reunite them, for sure.

If Dana is going to keep Hanna, She may need to get used to dry land for awhile," Braynar told her.

"That's true,"Danalli agreed. "Anyway, I feel the need to be close to the children myself. I feel like the babies are calling for me and can't shake it."

"Uh uh uh uhwah ! Uh uh uh uh wahaaaaaa! Wahhhahaha!"

"You're being paged," Braynar told Cecilia, then chuckled.

"Oh! Little girl! Eeew! Boys, please get a basin of water and some rags...." Cecilia told them....

Chapter 5

"The nurseries are all set up and ready. We made them as comfortable for the adults as we could, complete with feeding cages that load from the outside," Kenneth told Braynar.

"I'm really proud of you boys," Isabel told them. "Y'all have really stepped up to the plate. It does my heart good to know that the love you feel for her is really real and not based on lust."

"Who couldn't love her, mom? I mean, well..."

Keithen said.

"I know, sons. Let's bring them all in. I think we should let the babies see their new homes before we put them together. I don't want to overwhelm them." Isabel told them.

George came in first, carrying AlaHanDrea on his back, piggy back. She appeared to be the size of a 6 year old! She was only a couple of days old and was already a child!

"Wow! AlaHanDrea! Look at you! You're so big!" Braynar exclaimed!

"Ya, she had a growth spurt after breakfast," George replied.

"I should say she did!" Isabel exclaimed.

George put her down. Kenneth quickly changed her furnishings to be more suitable for a little girl. She looked at it all and ran over to Kenneth, climbing up him and put her arms around his neck for a hug. She squeezed him tight, then kissed him all over his face, telling him thank you, over and over as she kissed his face.

Kenneth giggled the whole time. "Oh,, baby girl, it was nothing. I've gotta take good care of my baby queen, now, don't I? I'm so happy you're here with us!"

He squeezed her back and twirled her in circles... Then put her down.

"I wubs you, Kennet," she told him.

"Ah, I love you, too, sweet girl! I love you, too!" Kenneth had tears rolling down his cheeks.

"Awe, don cwy, Kennet, I not be dead any more. I don like dead. We can keep my bwood in de fwidge for be sure I won be dead wong, it's o.k. Don cwy..."

"Their tears of joy, my baby love, they are tears of joy!"

"Kennet, when I fins growin, I kiss you wite, make you feew betta," she said, then kissed his cheek and hugged him again.

Isabel spoke to Danalli, Braynar and Keithen to where only they could hear, " I didn't even know that AlaHanDrea and Kenneth were a thing before this happened. Did y'all?"

They all shook their heads no.

"So, where's my baby girl?" Leon asked as he entered the room.

"Weon!" She squealed, as she ran and jumped in his arms. He hugged her tight, then sat her down, " Wow! Look at you! Wow!!!"

"Ya, I gwoing as fass as I can!"

"I see that!"

"So, where's my babies?" AlaHanDrea asked. "I wanna see my babies. Weon, I have chiwdwens, babies chiwdwens... 2 of dem!"

"You do?"

"Uh, I made a dem from my bwood... Aw by mysef."

"Wow! That's amazing!" Leon told her.

"They are here, sweet girl. They just arrived and are in their rooms. Just as soon as they get settled, you can see them," Isabel told her.

As soon as Isabel told her that, Tootsie brought Aleha out from her room and sat her down. AlaHanDrea ran over to her, then sat down in front of her.

Aleha sat up straight, smacking her legs with her hands and drooling, then laughed and reached for AlaHanDrea. "Mommy!"

Stunned silence filled the room when Aleha crawled into AlaHanDrea and vanished.

AlaHanDrea patted her chest, tears streaming down her face... She sat quietly, not moving, tears streaming down.

No one knew what to do! They didn't know what just happened or quite what to make of it... Aleha was just gone!

They waited to see if the baby had absorbed her mother, but it didn't appear so.

Isabel telepathically told Cathey Ann to take Hanna and run! Take her back to Dane and Dana and stay there until further word, then told Cathey Ann what happened with Aleha.

When she told Dane and Dana, they packed up and moved as quickly as they could. King Neptune put them on a remote island where they wouldn't be found. Where only he knew where they were.

"The only problem here, son, is that if AlaHanDrea wants her baby, or visa versa, they will summon one another, so, I'm putting up a shield over the island so the signals won't get through. But, neither will yours. Here, keep this monitor so you and I can keep in touch. We will have to rely on human technology to stay in touch," King Neptune told his son.

"Why do you think Aleha did that, daddy?"

"Who knows, son. Maybe they are not really her children. Maybe they are parts of her and she's pulling herself together, I don't know. I've never seen anything like this before in all my time..."

"Well, I think she's amazing. I will love and nurture this tiny one all I can, but guys, if this baby is part of AlaHanDrea, we have to return her. Also, we cannot let her die! If she's part of AlaHanDrea and she dies..."

"Oh! Right! I hadn't thought about that," Dane said.

"I love this baby and I Love AlaHanDrea, too. I want what's best for them both! For now, we can stay here and take care of this tiny one... But, we need humans to feed her or we will be eaten ourselves... Or, absorbed. She doesn't know not to.

Please don't forget how dangerous this baby is!" Neptune said.

"Bob." A voice said.

Startled, they all turned to look, it was Bob!

"Bob! How did you... Hi, good to see you!"

"Good to see you, too!" Bob told them.

"You took the baby. I felt you take her. She's mine."

"She's yours? I don't understand," King Neptune told him.

"I'm made from AlaHanDrea's DNA. From her cloned DNA. Baby is mine. I mean, she is mine to fix her. My language is still not so good," Bob told them.

"O.k. how did you find us?" Dane asked.

"Followed the baby. Baby called, I followed her call me."

"So much for the shields, dad," Dane said.

"Let me hold her," Bob said.

The baby vanished inside of Bob... They all stood in a near frozen panic... But the baby re appeared in Bob's arms. "Pretty baby, you're so beautiful. You can live now, pretty baby. Hanna baby. If you have Any problems, call for me and I will come fix. Go ahead, put shields up, they will work, just not to me." Bob told them, and handed the baby back to Dana.

"Don't let her go near AlaHanDrea, or she will join with her, like Aleha did."

"Bob, is this baby part of AlaHanDrea?" Dane asked.

"No. She is her daughter. But she will join with her mother, don't let her near AlaHanDrea. If you need me, I will come. I will come anyway for visits. If teeth hurt, I will come."

"Yes Bob, and thank you. Uh, Bob, what did you do to her?" Dane asked.

"I fixed her heart and her liver, so she won't die."

"Oh wow!

Bob!

Thanks man!" Dane said.

"She's mine to care for."

Bob said, then vanished.

"AlaHanDrea's going to know that we have her, it's her right to know," Dana said.

"True enough, but she doesn't need to know where you are," king Neptune told them. "Hanna should be o.k. now.

Bob said he fixed her. Let's get you kids settled. I will send Athena and Isabel by shortly.

Ya, Just try and keep her location a secret from those two!" Neptune told them, sarcastically....

"What do you think happened, George?" Isabel asked.

"I don't know.... Baby girl, can I sit by you for a minute?" George asked.

AlaHanDrea was still sitting on the floor, head hung low, tears running down her cheeks...

"Baby girl, what happened? Where did Aleha go?" George asked her.

"She was my daughter... My baby girl."

"Sweetheart, what happened?"

"She joined with me! Boooohoohoohoooohoooohoooo uh waaahahhaaaaaa....."

"Now, now, oh baby girl, I'm so sorry... Do you know why she would do that?" George asked her...

Ground fog and bright lights announced the arrival of an angel.

"Hello, I'm Sarafina. AlaHanDrea and Athena already know me. AlaHanDrea... Baby, it's me, Sarafina. Please baby girl, please come to me and allow me to comfort you..." George got up out of the way.

Sarafina went over and sat down next to the distraught little girl.

"Sarafina, why did Aleha do that? Why'd she do that?"

"Because you are regenerating, baby girl. You're being remade. At the time that your blood was taken, most of you was laying in a coma over the poison, so, the seeds grew what you need to regenerate. She joined with you to help heal you and help you to hurry and grow back into yourself.

You don't have to do childhood over again, sweetie, you'll be full grown again really soon.

You see, you have the ability to regenerate. It's part of your gift. If you were to bleed a whole lot, and many babies were to grow, they would all join with you to heal you faster. It's your way of regenerating. You see, the babies are all you. There is no father. They are putting you back together. Joining with you is what they have to do."

"Oh. But, I wanted to keep her."

"But, she wasn't that kind of baby. She served her purpose."

"What about Hanna?"

"Hanna has been interfered with. She has been taken and hidden away. She has been healed and is being taken care of by Dane and Dana. They are keeping her away from you so she won't join with you, because they don't understand her true purpose. They believe they are protecting her. They both love you very much and believe they are protecting her from you, for you."

"Will I get well and grow without Hanna?"

"Yes, sweetie, you will."

"If I don't see Hannah and I get well, and then I see her later, will she still join with me?"

"Yes, as soon as she sees you, she will run to join with you."

"So, Hannah's only chance at living by herself is to stay away from me?"

"Well, yes.."

"If she sees me, she dies..."

"No, not dies, joins together with you. Aleha is not dead, she's part of you now. More than if she were absorbed by you."

"But, she was my daughter!"

"Well, ya, in a sense, but only because she is your offspring, but, she grew for one reason and that was to heal you... Her whole purpose is to heal you! She's a necessary part of your rebirth."

"But, I want Hannah to live outside of me."

"Sweetheart, babies born of your blood, are born in order to make you stronger! They are little parts of you, grown to join with you and heal you! They are parts of you! Baby, they Are your Blood, not your eggs! Your eggs are your children, not your blood! Blood babies join with you, because they are you! Yes, technically they are your offspring, but differently from eggs. Eggs are made whole with a mother and a father. Blood seeds are parts of you, growing to make you stronger."

"Oh. So, I'm my blood babies and they are me, but my egg babies are from me and he... His and my babies. And Me babies are on purpose to join with me because they are drops of me..."

"Right. So, Hannah Has to join... It's what she's got to do. You should consider growing a dozen of them and finish getting grown up..."

"O.k. can Hannah stay with Dane and Dana if I grow more?"

"She can stay there for as long as you want, but know this, she wants and needs to join with you. If you allow her to grow up enough, she will hunt you down and join with you."

"Please, I want to grow as many as I need to be all grown up again..."

Chapter 6

"Merrill, how big are the pods?" Danalli asked the wizard...

"Look at them! They're growing really fast!

I've been feeding the vines all they can eat.

I found out by accident that the plant eats small animals... When it does, the pods growing speed increases drastically,"

"Are you ready to announce the pods opening yet?"

"Ya, we better go ahead and allow everyone to gather that want to assist..."

"Those drones are fast!" Merrill chuckled.

"We're here!" Tootsie and Cathey Ann announced.

Isabel, Athena, Braynar, Keithen, George, Raynar and Barbara we're right behind them.

"Don't start without us!" Healix and Jax said, as they walked in.

Kenneth, Brian, Franklon and Leon were about 2 minutes behind them. As were Paulio, Thomlin, Sam & Brian, & more than ready to stand guard...

King Neptune, King Bjorn, King William and King Leon were about 5 minutes behind them.

Then, the triplets arrived, with their husbands.

"We're ready," the triplets announced.

Two of Tootsies favorite she dragons, Felicia and Fannie, brought AlaHanDrea in... She was the size of a 9 year old child already.

The pods were beginning to have movement...

Thanks to the drones, the whole world watched, as the pods began to tear open... 22 pods, total, began breaking open to reveal babies, some as large as a 1 year old. Only a few were as tiny as newborn humans. Most of them were sitting up already, smiling and coooing...

All of them were hungry...

The humans prisons had offered up their first meals, so, the food wagons were all full.

The drones did not stop broadcasting while the babies enjoyed their first meals.

It unnerved most humans to witness other humans being consumed...

The world watched in utter amazement as AlaHanDrea went from baby to baby... Each of the babies eagerly joining with her... With each joining, AlaHanDrea grew larger, older, slowly but surely becoming the woman she was, prior to the poisoning... Prior to being murdered...

Dane and Dana brought Hannah, but, AlaHanDrea asked that she be kept away for a bit.

Hanna had begun growing quicker, once Bob repaired her .

"Dane," AlaHanDrea called out. He went over to her, without Dana and the baby.

"Dane, Bob wants Hannah.

Hannah is me.

Bob wants to absorb her, once she's bigger.

You won't be able to stop him.

No will be able to stop him.

None of you are safe as long as Hannah and I are separate.

Dane, I want Hannah to live her life separately, but she was created from me, for me.

Thank you Dane. Thank you and thank Dana for trying to protect her, keep her safe and raise her with love.

I'm sorry that she cannot be kept."

"She's you, AlaHanDrea, I can't help but to love her! Dana loves her because Dana also loves you! More than you know!

Yes, we're sad, but at the same time, we're glad... Glad that you are able to grow healthy parts of you in order to regenerate.

I'm afraid Neither of us was taking the news of your death very well.

No one was, really.

No one was...

The loss of Hannah is not a loss at all...... It's a gain. We have you back!"

"I don't much care for dead.

Alive is much better.

Dead has no body.

I rather enjoy having a body.

I would miss you too much, if I were to remain dead.

Thank you, all y'all, for helping me to no longer be dead.

Thank you, Merrill, for discovering the seeds in my blood and figuring out how to grow them...

Thank you, Sarafina for explaining it to me... Thanks to every one of you!

I need to finish growing, look at how big I am now!"

She continued to go from baby to baby...

So many pretty little baby girls, smiling, smacking their legs with their hands, blowing spit bubbles . Some were laying on their backs, chewing on their toes ... Until it was her turn, then, they'd sit up and reach for AlaHanDrea, then vanish in her.

AlaHanDrea would grow a little more...

The human population didn't much like the fact that humans were on the menu, but it didn't stop them from loving AlaHanDrea! The danger of her was the biggest part of her appeal!

Cheering could be heard getting louder with each joining, as the world watched the most incredible recreation of a life anyone had ever seen......

It's safe to say that the world was in Awe!

Dana finally brought Hannah out.

She was getting fussy, calling out Mommy, as loudly as she could, until she saw AlaHanDrea....

She laughed, reaching for her.

Once AlaHanDrea got over to her, Hannah didn't rush to join.

She sat, smiling at AlaHanDrea, then, they began to talk to each other, where Dane and Dana could hear... " We are parts of the same person, we belong together.

I AM living my life once we join, because we are the same person. Hannah stood up and hugged AlaHanDrea, then vanished into her.

Everyone gasped when AlaHanDrea fainted.

Danalli caught her before she hit the floor. He scooped her up into his arms and carried over to an exam bed.

Healix checked her out, as did Merrill.

She was in a coma.

Neither of them were quite sure why.

"This is pure speculation, here, but, it could be the final stage in her rejuvenation,"Healix told everyone, where the drones could clearly hear.

"All we can do now is to sit and wait..."

Mitchin pulled up a chair next her bed.

Braynar, Keithen, Kenneth and Danalli followed suit.

Everyone else produced a chair and had a seat, right where they stood.

Everyone just sat, staring....waiting.... Praying.... Hoping....

Thomlin came rushing in, "Your majesties, George & Isabel."

"What is it Thomlin?"

"There are some humans here to see you that I think you should talk to.... In Private..."

"O.K, let's go in the other room, show them in," Isabel told him.

"Sure, but Prince Braynar is going to want to hear this. Prince Danalli and Prince Keithen probably do as well, as does George. I'll show them in, your majesty...."

"I'm sorry, no drones right now..." Braynar said as he shut the door to keep the spies out.

The humans Thomlin took in were dirty and raggedy looking. It was a small group of women.

"How can we help you ladies?" Isabel asked them. The women were huddled together, looked scared silly.

"Your majesty, we have had a long, dangerous journey to get to you!... We walked the entire distance here... We came to ask for your help! We beg of you, your majesty, please help us!

Our children have been taken! Mostly our boys, but some of the girls, too. Some as young as nine or ten!

The rebels got them!

The resistance.

They are trying to rebuild and have stolen our children to turn them into soldiers!" The women cried.

Anger filled everyone in the room...

George called for the counsel to meet at once, especially Carl!

The group of grieving mothers were questioned extensively by the counsel.

"What do you plan to do about this, Carl?"

"Well, I believe we need to form a task force, made up of all species, to hunt them down, free the children and squash this resistance!"

"Hello, all, I am Prince Harmon, of the watchers. Folks call me Mr. Jax...

For those who are unaware, watchers relocate species to different planetary homes. If this resistance is so unhappy on Taurus 9, they are welcome to be relocated to a different world to live on.

We volunteer to move them...

They need only step forward.

We will put them in the transport tunnels and they will be in their new home within a few short hours... Otherwise, they can face the dragons..."

"If ya don't like it here, then leave.

Now." George said.

Isabel called her female troops. She felt this was a job for the lady warriors, the dragon riders... As well as the ladies riding big cats, wolves and bears... It was time for the girls to show their stuff!

The small group of distraught mothers were given rides back home, on the backs of dragons... They never dreamed they'd be riding through the air on the backs of those magnificent beasts!

The women spent their lives in fear of dragon kind, only to discover that everything they thought they knew about dragons was a lie.

Soaring through the air was beyond magnificent, only topped by the ride back to Drakonia to live a new life in a new land.

Chapter 7

The counsel reconvened to talk to Carl about the state of affairs with the resistance.

"Carl, dude, if you can't offer police to the poverty stricken population, then we will.

If you cannot manage to take care of your own population, then we are stepping in!

Humans are starving.

Creatures are not starving.

We take care of our own.

There is no such thing as a homeless dragon, unless a quake collapsed their home... In that case, they won't be homeless very long...

Queen AlaHanDrea has started a huge project, building entire towns dedicated to the raising of mostly human orphans, because humans don't take care of them.

The poverty stricken are being abused, misused and taken advantage of...

Our question for you is, why are their so many humans living in poverty? And why are most of the them women and children?

Carl, we are stepping in. If you won't cure these issues, the animal kingdoms will cure them for you!

We are taking the land we need..if someone objects, we will kill them.

We are coming to help.

Anyone who disagrees will be killed for ingratitude.

If you were capable of fixing it, the problem wouldn't exist.

But it does, so, we are stepping in.

This resistance isn't just against the animal kingdoms, it's against the poverty and injustice! So, we are stepping in to put an end to the nonsense.

We will try to have our citizens in human form mostly, but it won't always be possible, or practical..

Deal with it!

The children of kings from all species are volunteering to serve in your office. Make sure they receive due respect.

All complaints are being handled by the executioners...

Feel free to lodge all the complaints your little heart desires... To the executioners...

Meeting adjourned."

The monitors were switched off.

"Before everyone leaves, I'd like to suggest that King JayDe be placed in charge of the task force over the resistance, all in favor?"

There was a unanimous "I" ... "The I's have it! JayDe rules the task force against the resistance... JayDe!" George called out.

"Yes, your majesty?" JayDe asked.

"First of all, JayDe, when the counsel meets, you need to attend. You are, after all, a king. You... Are king over the werewolves.... As such, you need to be present at the council of Kings.

Now, with that said, in your absence, we took the liberty of voting you in charge of the task force over the resistance.

We're leaving it up to you to squash the resistance, King JayDe.

We can think of no one better suited for the job. We are confident that you will put an end to this ridiculousness.

Kill them, reform them, disband them, whatever you have to do. You can even turn them all into werewolves if you want to... and now, there's an idea!

Take the opportunity to expand your kingdom...

Just go bite them all!" George said in all seriousness.

"Pardon me, your majesty, but do you really want a bunch of werewolves running around loose in Drakonia?"

"Sure, why not?"

"When the moons become full, we have no control over the beast...
"

"The rest of the time, you have control?"

"Yes, your majesty."

"Then enact a law requiring your citizens to lock themselves in their escape proof cells at the local prisons, until the moon time is over... Huge problem, simple solution that actually cures another problem... and makes going to prison even more terrifying to the regular humans. Problem solved.

Just go bite them all!

Create your new kingdom.

Should things get out of hand, dragon kind will step in on your behalf.

Please be sure to release the kidnapped children to the royal guards for reprogramming... Think you can handle it? Because I have every confidence in you."

"Yes... Yes, your majesty. Wow! My life is SO different here on Taurus 9! I really LOVE IT HERE!"

Viewing screens popped up all over the human sectors.

"Greetings Human inhabitants of Taurus 9.

I... Am King JayDe, formerly of beta Centauri, now enjoying citizenship here on Taurus 9.

Due to 'the Resistance', as it likes to be called, a task force has been formed, of which, I am in control.

We have heard your reasons for forming and are determined to do what we can to correct the issues plaguing man kind.

I'm here today to tell you, that your tactics will not be tolerated.

You will disband at once. Failure to do so, will result in you having to deal with me.

I, am a werewolf. I was born a human. I became a werewolf when I pissed off a sorceress. A very powerful sorceress...

One bite from me, and you too will become a werewolf!

Disband or become as I am! Unless, of course, I decided to kill you instead.

It is doubtful that the human community will enjoy having werewolves among you. So, you may want to reconsider supporting the resistance.

Werewolves have no control during the moon cycle when they are at their fullest... We simply act on our bloodlust and kill whoever we see first.

Death by werewolf is not a fun way to die... very unpleasant, to say the least.

On beta Centauri where I'm from, terror filled the hearts of mankind during the moon cycle, knowing that the werewolves were going to roam.

I'm sure they were glad to get rid of me.

This problem can be avoided here on Taurus 9. If you end up with werewolves among you, you only have yourselves to blame, because you were given the chance to not have werewolves among you... with the exception of me, of course.

Squash the resistance and do it now, or pay the price... simple as that... this is the only broadcast that I'll be making. You've been told.

We, in the animal kingdoms, look forward to assisting mankind in curing your problems with poverty and the enormous amount of homeless orphans that you seem to have.

Hopefully, together, we can end starvation and poverty for you.

At least we're going to try.

Those of you in high crime areas, can look forward to that stopping.

This is just a heads up for the criminal element... We're coming for you!

Good day."

————————

"How is AlaHanDrea today?" Braynar, JayDe and Leon asked.

"There is no change," Healix answered.

Braynar took her hand in his... They all stood and watched while she got up, separating from her body again, physically, dividing again...while she remained on the table, in a coma...

The woman they had known, stood in front of them!

Fully grown!

She began stepping out of body after body until there were four. Braynar wasted no time pulling her into his arms, as did Leon and even JayDe went in for a quick hug.

Danalli, Keithen and Kenneth came walking in. She separated again, so she could hug them all at the same time. All of the men were extremely happy to see her! All but JayDe scooped one up in their arms and left with her...

Much to JayDe's amazement, there was one remaining...

"JayDe, we haven't had a chance to spend much time together. Would you like to spend some time with me?" She asked.

A big ol smile told her all she needed to know...

"Very much... Yes, I would like that very much..." He stepped over, took her face in his hands and kissed her lovingly. She smiled real big, then put her arms around him and kissed him back.

"Braynar, I'm a virgin again, sweetheart. I also plan to stay that way, at least for now," she told him, as well as the others. "Yes, I'm so happy to be back, I just don't want to have sex, yet. It complicated things.

I'm not ready to be a mother yet. I am, but I'm not. Sex makes babies. It just does."

"That's o.k. baby girl, I can respect that. Can we lay and cuddle? Can I hold you?"

"I would love that, Braynar! It was so strange being a baby again!"

"Oh, I'll bet! I must say, you look pretty good for a week old infant..." He teased....

She just smiled...

"You pitched some pretty good fits at me, there, young lady!" He teased.

"Ya, well, I was a newly born baby..."

"Yes you were and so precious, I might add!"

"Bray, thank you for taking such good care of me. You're a great dad! All of you guys did an outstanding job taking care of me while I was so tiny and helpless. I love the way males take care of the young! You guys all rock!"

"If we don't do it, who will, the women???" He chuckled..."ya, right ...

The women have enough to do without adding tending to the children to the list! Children are not easy, especially in a dangerous world! Children need their fathers every bit as much as they need their mothers!"

"I couldn't agree more!"

"Someday, I will be taking care of Our children.... Someday...

Sweet girl, may I please ask you a question? Why are you in a comma?

"Because I was poisoned."

"Right, but that body died and you were reborn."

"True, but I was already poisoned when my blood was drawn."

"Braynar got a sick feeling deep inside his gut.... " you're still in danger, aren't you?"

"Yes, I am."

Braynar sent telepathic messages to Isabel. She ran to Merrill to tell him why baby girl was in a comma....

Merrill very quickly began planting more seeds... then went back to researching how to adapt the antidote to work with AlaHanDrea's blood...

JayDe was happy to be spending time with AlaHanDrea. He only had to get slapped twice for touching where he shouldn't have been touching. That was pretty good for him, actually. AlaHanDrea just laughed with him over it.... He was glad she was able to find the humor in it all.

JayDe told her all about the resistance. She was excited for him and his new life. She knew what it was like to be rejected as a monster.... Life on Taurus 9 was much better.... For both of them....

"Girl, I'm totally blown away! Everyone hated me on Beta Centauri. Everyone feared me... feared my bite! But here, I'm respected!

Wanted!

Liked!

Maybe even... loved!

I have a job BeCauSe I'm a Werewolf!

I'm a fricking King!￼

I find myself embracing the wolf, the monster, inside! I find myself loving him...

I'm no longer miserable!

My curse has become a blessing!

I just had to get with folks that can appreciate me for who and what I am!"

"We have so much in common, JayDee! This is kinda weird, you met the mimic, made love to her, fell in love with her... true, she was pretending to be me, but you had never met me... you met, the imposter. II just look like her... because she looked like me... still, I'm not her.

You and I actually do have a lot in common... I just wish that we could have met without the mimic in the mix... "

"AlaHanDrea, the very things I loved about her.... Well, they aren't hers, their yours. I met you, before I met you. I got to know a lot about you, before I met you. My feeling are not for some mimic faking to be you! They are not! They are real and for you! I've watched you since you returned... I've studied you, girl, and one thing I do know, is that my feelings are for you and are true. That's Why I need to spend time with you... why I need the opportunity to court you & let you see if you might fall for me, too." He leaned in and kissed her tenderly, making sparks fly. The sparks began to ignite passion. AlaHanDrea suddenly vanished.

The guys all ran into each other arriving at Merrill's. They knew when the saw one another... they just knew....

Chapter 8

"Breaking News!

We've been covering the story of the teen queen, Queen AlaHanDrea.

We all watched in amazement at her rebirth and regeneration.

Unfortunately, the blood draw occurred after she was poisoned...

The coma was caused by the original poisoning.

It's with a heavy heart that we tell you, Today, Queen AlaHanDrea passed away, again.

More pods are being grown in anticipation of this occurring.

No one knows whether or not this attempt will be anymore successful than the last attempt, all they can do is to try.

We will keep you informed.

Today, the world is once again in mourning for the most incredible creature this world has ever known.

Please pray for her, I know that we will be...

Be sure and tune in for the births of the new pods, expected to occur later today..."

"All we can do is to hope And pray and continue to assist. Is everyone coming?" Isabel asked Braynar.

"Yes mother, everyone I spoke to said they were."

"Good, we'll be needing them all very shortly. We'd better get going ourselves," Isabel told her sons.

"It's just got to work this time, mom, it's just got to!" Keithen said, obviously distraught.

The drones were there when everyone began arriving, preparing for the rebirth.

No one was surprised.

Everyone was shocked when the first pod opened and the baby was tiny.

More like a newborn human baby.

The second pod was the same, and the third, fourth, fifth.....

Healix carried the first baby over to the second one, laying them side by side.

At first, nothing happened.

The babies just looked at one another. But then, one rolled over until she blended into the first one.

Cheers could be heard from all over!

Some of the pods were taking their sweet time at opening.

Merrill began to worry that if it didn't work that time, they'd lose her forever.

Then it hit him, draw blood from the reborn baby...

He began drawing blood from the umbilical cords... Saved birth fluids as well.

Sure enough, much to Merrill and Healix relief, seeds were present!

They were present in the placentas as well.

They planted the seeds while pods were still opening.

30 pods opened... 30 hours later, a full grown AlaHanDrea stood before them!

Healix had an idea....

Merrill, will the plant eat blood? Or does it want the whole animal?"

"That's a good question. Whatcha got in mind?"

"Here, draw some of my blood. Raynar, come here and roll up your sleeve..."

The plant sucked up the blood like it was the plants last meal! Then, they fed the placentas to the plants.

Pods began to rapidly grow, and large, too!

"AlaHanDrea passed out, just like the last time. And just like the last time, she stepped out of herself, only this time, she was weak and tired.

A few moments later, the copies vanished and the new body passed away.

The dragons and lions were beside themselves with grief.

Merrill and Healix rushed in to show everyone that newly born baby looking very much like a 1-year-old!

"Look what we grew! We used blood from the last bunch, then fed the plants watcher blood! And look!"

Merrill bragged.

AlaHanDrea was reaching out for Braynar to take her.

"My Bwwaynarse! An my isbes an kiefkins an my dawawawai! Kenit! Jorjeeee! Waynarse! Kwaiganse! Me ba gin!

Misser szzax!"

"Hello baby girl! Look how big you are!" Braynar said.

"I swong.dis tines... Where de udder ba?"

"O.k, we will take you back in there. We just wanted you to say hello. Would y'all like to come watch?" Healix asked.

Of course, everyone followed them...

The pods were all open by the time everyone went back in. After the third one, AlaHanDrea looked like a 7 year old! She was fully grown by number 12, but continued to join until all 36 were together.

She got stronger after each joining! But, once again, after the last pod, she slipped into coma...

8 copies stepped out that time.

It was looking good for a few days before they all vanished again. The new pods were already breaking open when her new body passed away

The baby of the first pod was the size of a toddler!

20 pods grew that time.

Once she had joined with the last one, she stepped out of herself, over and over again, but the first one didn't pass out like the times before!

20 AlaHanDreas stood before them, all strong, all appearing healthy! All smiling and chatting with other creatures.

Cheers could be heard raising up from all over the globe!

The first AlaHanDrea stepped forward to make an announcement... " "May I have everyone's attention please?

On this day, we have all witnessed a true miracle! A Miracle of epic proportions!

No, not my rebirth and regeneration...

Well, o.k., that, too...

I speak of a different miracle!

A watcher and a wizard worked together for a common goal!

And

It was Love that brought them together... Their mutual love for Me... Their desire to save me over powered their feelings for one another, allowing them to work side by side towards a common goal.

How about that! Love DOES conquer all!

Thank you, to my heros! As well as to all of my heros!

With all of my heart, I, uh, we, thank you!!!

The applause and cheers were deafening...

20 AlaHanDreas took a bow, then stepped inside one another just to step back out again.

They all laughed, then rejoined again. Everyone cracked up laughing.

The men all started going over to say hello, as they did, she'd separate and the copy would go with him.... or her, as the case was... Tootsie and Cathey Ann were right there for their own copy.

They were all her, all versions of her...

When she saw JayDe, she jumped out of herself and ran over to him.

"JayDe, so great to see you, let's get away from here..." she told him.

JayDe transformed, put her on his back, spread his wings and took off!

It was the first time she had ridden on a flying werewolf! She loved sitting above his wings, more on his shoulders than his back. His wings made him fly more like a bird of prey than a dragon. He soared a lot, tho, like dragons did.

Every time JayDe would fly down low, she'd do her battle call, "yeyeheeeyeyeyeyeyeyeyeyeiiiii". They'd hear cheers from the ground, energizing them as they flew...

JayDe finally began to tire, so he headed for a nearby island. When they landed, AlaHanDrea had him land on a peak, like a dragon would, then got down, went over and struck the gong 3 times, paused, then struck it 3 more times. The sound of rhythm drums told her message received.

She explained the practice to JayDe. He was thrilled to hear that food was coming. Of course, he was more into the killing than the eating, but he was still hungry. He just preferred animal flesh for eating. He killed humans, because that's what werewolves did...

Much to his delight, the natives brought a roasted pig.

AlaHanDrea heard gongs ringing out from several mountain peaks, thrilled that others had come to the same island!

Her and JayDe were shown to their hut. It came with 2 separate bedrooms, but they were sharing the same hut. They didn't mind.

"JayDe, it's only fair of me to tell you that I'm a virgin again."

"Oh, you are? O.K, so, that means, behave yourself, JayDe... got it!" He chuckled. "Ya know, where I'm from, we handle the whole virgin thing differently than they do here.

There's no procedure or dilators.... "

"But, isn't that painful?"

"Ya, I've heard it is, but only for the first few times or so…"

"I think I'll pass, thank you. I'd rather not have any negative experiences in that department."

"Suit yourself, of course, there are other things that we can do," the hopeful werewolf said, then kissed her very sweetly. Sparks flew like crazy!

A loud clap of thunder made them both jump! AlaHanDrea got very excited! JayDe didn't want to turn her lose, but she took off for outside anyway.

He had not ever witnessed her absorbing lightening before.

JayDe watched in utter amazement, as did a broadcast drone, as AlaHanDrea positioned herself on the nearest hill… she raised her arms and began calling the storm!

The whole world watched in utter amazement as lightening bolt after lightening bolt struck and were consumed until the entire storm seemed to vanish into her!

That was probably the quietest that planet had ever been!

Everyone was speechless!

The silence seemed to last forever, before the cheers began!

Once the storm was consumed, she threw her fists up in a victory stance and called out, "QUEEEEEN ALAHANDREAAAAAAA!!!!!!" The whole world cheered!

She had never felt so powerful….

AlaHanDrea put a small tent type cover over herself, then peed a stream from consuming that storm, then burped and said, "Scuse me!" and giggled, just like she always did.

The world had a whole new respect and understanding of the creature named AlaHanDrea after that day.

All of the other AlaHanDreas that had traveled to the island on the backs of dragons ran down to the beach. JayDe's version ran out to catch up with them. All of them became one. 12 joined on the beach. Dragons, shifted to human form, stood, feeling a bit disappointed that their copies joined into one. "I'm tired and want to go home." Is all she said before vanishing. Everyone rushed back to make sure she was o.k.

But, she was not.

By the time they arrived back at Merrill's, she had passed away, again.

"We were almost successful!

Almost!

This time, I'm administering the antidote for the poison.

That time, they had to wait for the pods to open. It seemed to be taking an awfully long time, that time.

Time seemed to be at a crawl, as everyone sat, waiting......

Merrill was feeding the vines, and feeding the vines...

Finally, Raynar, Jax and Healix father appeared, offering already drawn blood donations from many watchers, including from the council of grandfather's...

The plants sucked it all up like they hadn't been fed in a month!

Mitchin was next.

He had to allow the blood to be drawn, but Merrill couldn't touch the angel, not even in human form!

Healix drew the blood for him.

The plants almost attacked Healix to get at the angels blood!

All of a sudden, a pod began to open, finally!

There was a small child inside. She was about the size of a four year old! She got up, went over to the next pod, separated the pods leaf covering and said peekaboo! The pod opened and the child inside vanished into the first one! Within 5 pods, AlaHanDrea was fully grown!

She continued to join, opening pod after pod until 24 were opened and joined.

No one made a sound.

No one assisted with any births, or helped in any way. AlaHanDrea did it all herself.

Merrill took her blood.

When he looked that time, he couldn't find even a trace of the poison.

"I'm healed," was all she said, then quietly walked out of the room and faded out until she vanished. No one knew where she went, all they knew was that she went.

It had been nearly a week and there was no sign of AlaHanDrea.

There was also no trace of a dead body.

They were left to assume she was alive somewhere.

Chapter 9

"Good morning George, Raynar, Barbara. How are y'all this morning?" Isabel asked.

Everyone mumbled, "fine..."

"I had the strangest dream about AlaHanDrea.

Very strange.

She's hiding.

Gaining her strength back without all of the attention."

"I can feel her," Barbara said. "I've been able to feel her since she changed me.

She's hiding from Bob, mostly.

She says that no one can stop him.

He wants to absorb her and no one is powerful enough to stop him, maybe not even her.

Apparently, I will be going to join her to protect...." Barbara vanished!

"What the..." George started to say...

"Bob." Was all Bob said when he appeared.

"Oh, hello Bob, it's so good to see you again," Isabel said.

"Barbara?"

"She isn't here, Bob."

"Bob."

"Yes, I understand you want Barbara, but she isn't for you to absorb, simply because she has some of AlaHanDrea in her...

You mustn't absorb her, Bob."

"Bob."

"I'm sorry Bob, she isn't for you. Neither is AlaHanDrea."

"Bob, AlaHanDrea, Bob."

"Bob, you speak better than this, what's happened to your ability to speak the language?" Isabel asked.

"Bob. Bob kiwi apple kiwi apple apple kiwi Bob."

"Oh, wow Bob, I'm so sorry to hear that. Guys, he's digressing. He's afraid he may be dying."

"Wait, you understand him?" George asked.

"Yes, don't you?"

"Uh, no."

"Bob, you need to see Healix and Merrill. But Bob, you must not kill or absorb Healix or Merrill. Merrill may be able to fix you the same way he fixed AlaHanDrea.

Would you like for me to go with you?" Isabel asked him.

"Bob."

"O.k., but Bob, you must not absorb me either! I will help you, but you cannot absorb me! Got it? "

"Bob."

"C'mon, let's go. Shift to dragon and we'll fly, because I'm not carrying you, Bob."

"Bob, Isabel, Bob Bob Bob..."

"Thank you, Bob, now, let's be on our way, follow me..."

"Nanner Nanner, Isabel, Bob Bob..."

"Thank you, Bob. I love you more than bananas, too."

"Merrill? Are you around? Is Healix here by chance?" Isabel hollered out.

Healix popped in when he heard her calling out his name, then Merrill came walking in.

"Good morning your majesty," Merrill said, as he greeted Isabel.

"Good morning, how's my favorite sister in law?" Healix asked.

"Merrill, please allow me to introduce you to Bob. Human scientists created him attempting to recreate AlaHanDrea. Bob has a serious problem. For some reason, he is digressing and is afraid he is dying." Isabel explained.

"Bob."

"Hello Bob, nice to meet you," Merrill said, shaking Bobs hand.

"Bob nanner nanner kiwi Bob."

"There's no reason to be afraid, Bob, I'm going to try my best to take good care of you. How long have you been like this?" Merrill asked him.

"Bob Bob nanner kiwi apple"

"O.k. well, relax. Now, I'm going to have to take a little blood out using a syringe and it may sting a little, but it only hurts for a moment, while I collect the sample. You have the seeds of life in your blood, if you are like AlaHanDrea. We are going to grow little baby Bob's that will join with you and make you all better"

"O.k."

"Very good, Bob!"

"Uh, Merrill, I think it's only fair to warn you, Bob doesn't normally look like he does right now. His natural form can be a bit disturbing."

"Duly noted," Merrill told her.

"Merrill, I must say that I'm impressed. You understand Bob's language." Isabel told the wizard.

"It's a gift," Merrill replied.

"There, now, that didn't hurt too much, did it, Bob?"

"Bob."

"Bob, I'm going to sit and visit with Healix for a bit. I'm not going anywhere. I'm right here with you. You're in good hands and I'm just right here in the next room."

"O.k."

"Thank You, Merrill."

"Don't mention it. He'll be just fine, although I believe he's going to stay here with me for a bit. Would you like that Bob?"

"Yes."

"Very good, Bob! Ok , but, I'm still going to stick around for a little bit until we know something." Isabel told him.

Isabel and Healix waited together until Merrill needed to consult with Healix. After close examination, they determined that Bobs cells were beginning to break down.

It seemed the humans didn't do the greatest job creating Bob. His cell structure wasn't holding up.

Within 3 hours of arriving at Merrill's, Bob passed away.

They tried to revive him, but it was useless. His blood did not contain sufficient seeds of life for regrowing parts in order to repair him.

He was lab created, not creature created.

Try as he may, man is not capable of creating life as good as nature does it.

"I'm so sorry, Isabel, Bob didn't make it."

"What? Bob's dead? But how, why? Was there nothing that could be done to save him?"

"I'm afraid not. His cell structure failed to hold.

He began shifting in all of the wrong directions. Trust me, you don't want to see him!" Healix told her. " We used magic to place him in a crate. He's a real mess, Isabel."

"Oh, poor Bob! He told me he was afraid he was going to die. He was so scared. He came by wanting to absorb Barbara!

Thankfully, she was gone.

Bless his heart. I didn't see his spirit..."

"He was taken up before his body was finished doing what it was doing.... " Merrill explained.

"Oh my.

AlaHanDrea!" Isabel called out, summoning her...

Isabel finally sent her a telepathic message telling her that Bob had passed away.

The flock over heard it and within a very short time, wizards keep was over run with dragons....

Dragons mourning the passing of a creature they had all fallen in love with and accepted into their flock....

Bob would be missed....

Chapter 10

Bob had touched so many lives! He had an innocence about him that made creatures gravitate to him.

Everyone was in shock that he was gone.

Grief was not something dragons were accustomed to dealing with.

Tootsie took the news of his passing especially hard.

She had real love for Bob. Too much to share him with someone destined to be the mother of his children, or, so they thought, because of Folica... ...

AlaHanDrea couldn't believe he was gone, either. His death was doing a real number on her head.

"Baby girl, I want you to think about something. The babies in the pods were born looking like baby you. Just like baby you. They did not look like Bob. I believe that your mother lied to you," Isabel told her.

"Merrill tried to grow baby Bob's, they looked like Bob in his natural form. Your babies looked like baby you!"

"But, why would my mother lie to me like that? I don't understand?"

"I'm not sure why your mom has done any of the things that she has done.

It's as if she's going out of her way to make you feel badly about yourself. I'm guessing here, but maybe she's actually lying to herself, attempting to justify her suicide..."

"Sounds reasonable .. I'm trying really hard not to be too upset at her... I don't want to hate her, it's not good for me...

I really don't want to hate either of them, but, Isabel, they murdered me! Look what they put everyone through! They almost succeeded in making me forever dead! My own parents!"

"I know sweetheart."

Isabel sat down and cradled her in her arms, tears running down her face, crying with AlaHanDrea, gently rocking...

(They had become oblivious to the broadcast drones...)

The whole world wept with her...

Those who didn't think they liked the Teen Queen before the poisoning, fell in love with her, as she struggled to survive... Her popularity skyrocketed...

―――――――――――

" So, George, what to do about Folica and Jefry...." Raynar said...

"I don't know, truthfully. Jefry made some very valid points..."

"That may be true, but someone on this planet will kill them for what they did to Baby Girl, if we don't. Should I ask permission to relocate them to a new world?"

"That may be our best option... Exile them...."

―――――――――――

"Healix, come see this! It's Bob's pods! I adapted the food supply... messed with the seeds a bit, used some of AlaHanDrea's seeds for splicing, and... well.... You've gotta see this!"

""Hello, Merrill. Now, what's going on?"

"I adapted the food supply, made a couple of changes, magically, and, well, check this out... It's Bob, only better... Flaws repaired."

"What about his consciousness?"

"Well, I'm not big on talking to the guy upstairs, what's more, I'm not sure He'd listen if I did, but, you are on a first name basis with the Dude.... Chat with him? Please?"

"Merrill, He already knows. He already knows... AlaHanDrea and Bob get his attention...

Let's see what happens when the pods open..."

Healix telepathically called Raynar and Jax, filling them both in.

"Isabel, George!"

"What is it, Raynar?"

"Bobs pods are growing... successfully! All hands on deck, again..." Raynar told them.

"Merrill, we're all here! Merrill! Dude, where'd he go? Merrill?" George called out.

When they entered the chamber with the plants, they found Merrill struggling, with vines wrapped all around him. The plants were trying to eat him!

They rushed to free him, trying not to hurt the pods ... As others showed up, they joined the struggle!

The vines were everywhere! They were wrapping around everyone who went in!

AlaHanDrea walked in and all of a sudden, the plants turned everyone loose, retreating to the pots, making a whining sound....

Everyone was coughing and choking, some had a few minor injuries...

Isabel, Tootsie, Cathey Ann, George, Raynar, Barbara, Keithen, Braynar, JayDe, Danalli, Franklon, Paulio, Brian, Craigen, Merrill, Healix, Leon, Bjorn, William, Kai,, Dane, Neptune and Athena had all been wrapped in those carnivorous Vines! AlaHanDrea only had to walk into the room and they all retreated!

"Are Y'all all O.K.? What's going on?" AlaHanDrea asked, voice full of concern.

"I think we are all o.k. Those are some dangerous vines! Not like yours, baby girl! You and he are Not the same creatures! Apparently, Bob is part Mimic," Merrill told her. " Whoever told you that y'all were the same, is a liar."

"Is Bob regenerating?" She asked.

"Yes, I believe that he is. I think we achieved success..." Merrill told her.

"The pods are huge!" Isabel remarked.

Raynar walked over to a pod, laid his hand on it and made images appear on a viewing screen...

They all watched as the Blob baby inside shifted to a human looking creature... Sucking it's thumb...

Raynar stepped over to another pod, it was the same, the babies shifted to a more human looking form...

Still, everyone decided it best to allow things to occur more naturally, rather than to risk injury or worse... Only AlaHanDrea remained in the room.

The pods finally opened. The first baby did like AlaHanDrea did, going from pod to pod, joining, eagerly, one at a time...

The finished result shifted from natural, back to humanoid to natural and back again before remaining humanoid.

He tilted his head back and hollered out, "BOB!!!"

Bob finally spotted AlaHanDrea standing over by the wall, barely visible, smiling. "Hello Bob, my brother... I'm so happy to see you! I wasn't handling losing you very well," AlaHanDrea told him. He started for a hug, but, she had her shields up... "The hugs will wait until after you've absorbed something and eaten... Love ya, bro!"

"You don't trust me," Bob told her.

"Quite the contrary, Bob, I trust you completely. That's why my Shields are up! I trust you to be exactly who and how you are."

"Ya. O.k., Ya."

"Welcome back, bro, welcome back," she said with a smile.

Chapter 11

The sound of rhythm drums filled the early evening air...

AlaHanDrea laid, relaxing in the gentle breeze, in her hammock, listening to the music.

The most beautiful male voice she had ever heard began singing... "She's everything to me, call me silly, call me Craaaazy.... She's everything to me.... She's everything to me.... My Tootsie .... My sweet... my beautiful...... Tootsie..... She's everything to me..... Call me silly... Call me Craaaaaazy... She's everything to me.....she's my Tootsie...... Come back, come back, come back to me... Come back....come back... Come back... My Tootsie.... My beautiful Tootsie...

I came back, came back , came back for you ... Won't you come back, come back, come back to me.... my Tootsie..... My beautiful Tootsie... she's everything to me......call me silly.... call me Craaaaaazy... She everything to me!"

The sound of applause and Bobs silence, told AlaHanDrea that Tootsie shut him up with a kiss....... She just smiled, feeling good about Bob and Tootsie getting back together, now that she knew AlaHanDrea wasn't destined to be the Queen to Bobs King.

Tootsie and Bob made such a beautiful couple!

Bob was a very handsome man in human state. Tall, broad shoulders, very muscular and strong, golden blonde to platinum blonde hair, crystal grey blue and golden eyes, tanned complexion.... With a voice that could melt the coldest heart.

Tootsie was a very lucky girl, for sure! What a catch was he!

Bob seemed different when he regenerated. More sure of himself, stronger, more confident and more capable.

The very traits that also made him a whole lot scarier!

"Penny for your thoughts," Danalli said, startling her.

"Danalli! Hi, baby!"

"Hi yourself. How ya feeling, girl?".

"I dunno, Danalli. It's hard to come to terms with it all... and now, I have to make a decision about sending my parents into exile or executing them."

"But, isn't your mind already made up?

You chose exile, right?

I can't see you ordering the execution of your own parents. It would haunt you for the rest of your days...

I naturally assumed you had already chosen exile."

"I suppose. Either choice doesn't feels good."

"I'm sure none of it feels good, baby girl."

"You're right."

"Hey, c'mon, scooch over, I'm a big fella and need some room, if I'm going to climb in there and join you..." He reached down and scooped her up in his arms, then began singing to her.... With her in his arms and with him singing to her, he straddled the hammock, then laid down in it without missing a note.

AlaHanDrea loved how physically in shape Danalli was. He had amazing control over his own body.

Acrobatics came easy to him....

He sang her the most beautiful song of a love so true.... Laying in that hammock, leaning over her... At the end of the song, he kissed her so lovingly she melted in his arms...

A fire lit deep within her.

When she came to again, she was laying on a doctor's table...

It only took her a moment to realize what had happened to her...

Danalli put her to sleep and performed a Hymonectomy on her!

"That sly dog..." She said, smiling...

"You're awake! A little sooner than I expected, hello there...

The procedure went fine. I removed that nasty little piece of skin for you.

I don't want my sweetheart in pain..."

"I love you, Danalli. How long before it heals?"

It shouldn't take too awfully long. Tell me something, are you also with Leon, Braynar, Keithen, Kenneth, JayDe, etc... Tonight? Or, is this all of you?"

She looked up at him smiling.... "Ya, I'm out visiting.... But, I stayed home just for you."

"I hope you know how hard it is for me to not just...... Oh, my sweet baby girl....thank God we don't have to wait for you to grow up again! " He scooped her back up in his arms, stretched out his wings , flying off with her, back to her place.

She loved it when he only partially shifted...

She especially loved it when he kissed her while flying with her in his arms...

She caught herself wondering what it would be like to wrap her legs around him and do stuff while he was flying....."baby girl, as great as that sounds, I'd most likely crash!" He laughed. "Ya, I heard those thoughts! Loud and clear! Actually, I think the whole flock heard those..." He laughed!

The broadcast drones didn't follow Danalli because he used magic to insure their privacy, but once they returned, they were on again... under the eye of the drones...

Those tiny drones had a way of staying out of sight... They made you forget they were there.

The whole world was enjoying watching AlaHanDrea living her life as if no one was watching....

Before long, it became common for viewing screens to stay up showing poll results over all sorts of stuff. Everyone seemed to have an opinion over stuff in her daily life... Those opinions were reflected in the pole results...

2,686,316,243 believed she should go ahead and sleep with Danalli...

While, 32,624,557,892.1 believed she should wait.

AlaHanDrea thought the polls were funny most of the time. Sometimes, she actually appreciated seeing others opinions.

39, 974, 922, 567 agreed that she should send her parents into exile.

264, 992 thought her parents should be executed.

167 felt that her parents should be fed to the dragons.

16 felt that her parents needed psychiatric care.

Her parents being exiled and receiving psychiatric care was unanimous.

"JEFFRY, THEY ARE GOING to kill us! What are we going to do? We can't just sit here and wait for death to come!"

"Folica, we did nothing wrong, baby."

"We killed our own child."

"Well, of course we killed her, look at all the trouble she caused... had it not been for her, you and I would not have broken up and you wouldn't have killed your self!"

"But... if it hadn't been for her, we'd all be dead right now. She's the one that warned everyone about the galaxies colliding. Trillions of lives were saved by her warnings.

"Oh. Ya, I didn't think about that. Hmmm. Maybe I should have thought about that. Maybe we shouldn't have killed her. But, Folica, how were we supposed to begin again with her around as a constant reminder of our mistakes?"

"Ya, but, killing her doesn't erase our memories of her. She's dead and we still know we had her. We still went through everything we went through. All we accomplished by killing her was making her dead, and she's our child! Our new babies sister!"

"You mean, our future babies sister..."

"No, I mean, our babies sister."

"Folica, Folica, you mean, uh, you , uh, ya mean, uh, uh, ya mean... uh...."

"Yes. That's exactly what I mean,"

"Well, can't you get rid of it?"

"Why would I want to do that?"

"Because we don't want a baby right now."

"Then maybe you shouldn't have put a baby in me!"

"But, it feels real good, Folica. Why can't you stop it from making a baby, it's your body! Can't you just flush it out or something?"

"Seriously, Jeffry?"

"Ya, seriously, Folica! I don't want to stop sexing with you! I shouldn't Have to stop sexing with you! That's so not fair, Folica! You're being so selfish!"

"What? How am I being selfish?"

"By not flushing the thing out. Just get rid of it. Kill it before it's born so it's not a baby yet."

"Jeffry, it's always a baby. It's not something weird that turns into a baby when it leaves my body, it's always a baby... when it's made, it's a baby. It's just not a born yet baby."

"So, you can't kill it before it grows and gets born?"

"No, Jeffry.

It's already a baby. It's already alive, it's just forming, so it can grow and be born."

"Don't I get a say in this?"

"Of course you do, you had 100% say in this! YOU PUT THE BABY IN ME, Jeffry!

I didn't do it by myself!

You KNEW what you were doing would put a baby in me, you did it anyway.

You made your choice when you chose to put your baby in my body!

You've had your say!

Killing it now or killing it once it's grown is the same, Jeffry.

Dead baby is dead baby, no matter its age when you make it dead.

You already know this, why am I having to tell you this?"

"Breaking News:

According to drone recordings, Folica and Jeffry, the parents of Queen AlaHanDrea, are expecting another child!

That's right!

Folica is pregnant by Jeffry, again!

Jeffry does not appear happy about the upcoming birth of his second child by Folica.

He was recorded as having asked her to just get rid of it, flush it out....

Folica said no!

She seems to regret their decision to kill their first born and is refusing to kill the unborn child, much to the disappointment of it's father.

Folica actually committed suicide when AlaHanDrea was only 2 days old.

AlaHanDrea saved her spirit, somehow. Later on, and not so long ago, a young lady had an accident. Her body survived, but she was gone. Somehow, Folica's spirit was transferred into the body of that young lady.

What this means is, the baby won't be like Queen AlahanDrea. The new body was that of a feline which shape shifts. 1 single species.

It would seem that Jeffry does not enjoy having children.

Maybe he should consider that before spreading his seed around!

With no bad intensions, I must say, Folica and Jeffry do not seem to possess the intelligence required for making sound decisions.

Therefore, the polls are reopening on the subject of what to do about the murder of teen queen, Queen AlaHanDrea.....

By the way, this reporter is very thrilled about the regeneration of Queen AlaHanDrea! Oh, how I wish humans were capable of doing that!

Let's see how the teen queen feels about all of these new events...."

———————

"AlaHanDrea! AlaHanDrea, have you seen the news?" Cathey Ann asked as she hurried into the teen Queens camp. "Oh, hello Danalli. I'm sorry, I didn't mean to disturb you.... Have y'all seen the news broadcast? The drones broadcasts?"

"No, why...?" AlaHanDrea asked.

"I think you should... Well, maybe I should just tell you...

"Go ahead..."

"Well, it's about your parents. There is just no easy way to say this... Folica is pregnant and Jeffry wants her to destroy it, only she's not having it." Cathey Ann told her.

"Oh my... Oh my... Oh...."

"Alaha, I'm sorry to be the one to upset you," Cathey Ann told her.

"Why do you call me Alaha?"

"Because your name is long and it's as beautiful as you are. Some refer to you as Drea. I prefer Alaha."

"I've heard them used before... was just wondering why."

"Do you mind?"

"No, not at all. Call me what you like ... so, I'm to have a sister..."

"Or Brother..."

"Can't say as I like this news much."

"I'm so sorry "

They don't need another child they think they have a right to murder.

They shouldn't be exiled until the child is born.

I should take the child, but, I don't really want it. But, what choice do I have, but to protect it from them? Oh my....."

Chapter 12

"Dana?

To see me?

O.k. show her in," AlaHanDrea said to Cathey Ann.

"She will see you now, but Dana, please don't say anything to upset her. I'm not sure why you're here, but please, she's been through enough," Cathey Ann told her.

"I'm not here to upset her, quite the opposite," she replied.

"Dana! Hello there, nice to finally get a chance to visit with you, please, come on in. Have a seat. Now, what can I do for you?" AlaHanDrea said to her.

"Alaha, uh AlaHanDrea, I'm here so you can get to know me better. If it's ok with you, I'd like to hang out for awhile, like, maybe, a week or so?"

"Is everything alright with you and Dane?"

"Oh, yes, Dane and I are fine. I need you to get to know me.

You see, I heard about what's going on, when I watched the broadcast.

I don't normally watch it, but was overhearing gossip..."

"O.K?"

"I'm assuming that you don't want those two raising a child...

Your parents, I mean...

I'm here to let you know that Dane and I will gladly step up and raise the child for you, if you wish."

"That would mean the two of you moving in with me..."

"O.K.?""

"You must know that Dane and I have been in love with one another since we were babies. He helped me learn to walk..."

"Yes, I do know that. I'm quite a bit older than Dane.

I remember that. I remember watching the two of you for Athena...

I remember your birthday, when he sang to you.

His love for you is one of the reasons I convinced Dane to marry me."

"It is? I'm confused."

"I have loved and admired you since I first saw you as an infant.

Not like a man loves a woman, but the love like a dear friend.

I'm loyal to you and if needed, would lay down my life for you."

"Thank you, Dana. I don't quite know what to say?"

"I'd like for you to have a chance to know me better, before making up your mind."

"Truthfully, I don't know what to say, or think... about a bunch of stuff..."

"Wanna go for a swim?"

"Maybe later."

"May I call you Alaha? Or, Drea?"

"Suit yourself. What do most call me?"

"Well, when they are talking about you as a warrior, they call you Drea. Otherwise, they call you Alaha." (Ah lay hù)

"O.k., well, both or neither..."

"Are you o.k? You don't seem o.k."

"Ya, I'm o.k."

"I don't mean to disturb you, but Prince Leon is here to see you," Cathey Ann told her.

She just sighed, then said to tell him that she was resting.

Leon was confused.

"When did you become Royal Guard, Cathey Ann? Not that there's anything wrong with it, I just didn't know.... Uh... That females... Well ..."

"Yes, Prince Leon, princesses are also guards, or, can be... Our choice. Right now, she needs female guards... So, naturally, I'm here for her."

"I meant no offense... "

"I'm sure, none taken..."

"Please don't take this wrong," he said, then took her in his arms, kissing her with passion. She was stunned, melting in his arms, becoming lost in that incredible kiss... then passed out from the medicine Leon had on his lips.

He laid her gently in a hammock, then entered AlaHanDrea's chamber.

Leon took a cloth from his pocket and washed his lips.

Then, he raised his hand towards Dana, causing her to not be able to move more than her eyes.

AlaHanDrea began to object, then Leon took her in his arms and kissed her with love and passion. She began to struggle against his hold on her, then melted in his arms, as sparks flew....

Leon scooped her up in his strong arms and kissed her again, before walking off with her.

As soon as they were out of site, Dana could move again and Cathey Ann woke up.

"Should we be worried?" Dana asked Cathey Ann.

"Not at all! That man can kiss!!! Wow! Wow! I mean, wow! What a kiss! Mmmmm, mmmm, mmm..."

Dana laughed... Feeling a tad bit jealous that he didn't choose to knock Her out with a kiss.

Leon was an extremely handsome and sexy Prince...

As a lion, he was magnificent!

Dana figured no woman could resist him!

She wasn't wrong!

"Leon, you bad boy, you knocked out my guard and stole me."

"Yes, I did. Do you object?"

"Do you care if I do?"

"Not particularly."

Leon said, as he began opening her top, then pulled her close and kissed her again, holding her hands behind her back in one of his hands.

"Leon, what are you doing?"

"What I should have done a long time ago..." He used a cloth to tie her elbows together behind her back.

"Uh, Leon..." She started to object...

Objecting left her mind almost immediately... his touch sent electricity coursing through her! He sensed a drone, flicked his hand and sent it flying, out of control, until he heard it smash against a tree, all the while, kissing her neck... not pausing for even a moment.

"WELL, IT WOULD SEEM that Prince Leon wasn't too keen on having us watch!" The reporter laughed.

"The polls are open!

How many believe that Prince Leon just took her virginity?

How many think she stopped him?

How many of you ladies wish Prince Leon had taken yours?

How many of you men wish Prince Leon was gay?

I'm not in the least bit gay and I wouldn't tell him no!

How many think Cathey Ann will be dreaming about that kiss for a very long time?

"HEY, LEON, YOU HOME, buddy?" Braynar called out. He got a loud roar as an answer.

(Of course, the drones were watching...)

"Yo, dude, it's me, Keithen, dude, Danalli's here, too, open up!" They all laughed.

Another roar made them all bust out laughing...

"Yeeeeessss?" Leon asked, as he opened the door, dressed to the nines...

"Wow! Don't you look stunningly amazing! Where you heading, Prince big kitty?" Keithen asked...

"Let me guess, you three are here, because you heard I took AlaHanDrea... Well, aren't y'all special, worrying about her flower being picked... So protective of y'all!" He joked.

"Well, where is she?" Braynar asked.

"Not real sure, bro. My guess is, at her house...."

"What, she's not here?" Danalli asked.

"No, dude, she was here, we were kissing, then she vanished, just like that!" Leon explained.

Fear gripped the trio when they heard him say that!

The four of them rushed to Merrill's house...

"Athena, you think Isabel did the right thing?" AlaHanDrea asked her.

"Well, I don't know about Athena, but I believe I did the right thing..." Isabel told her. "Those guys need to back off and give you some space!"

"That Leon is mighty yummy, Isabel!" AlaHanDrea told her.

"Well, I can't argue with you there!

But, Just what you need, a litter of kittens..." All three woman laughed over that one.

Isabel finally showed some mercy to the guys, and sent them a telepathic message that the baby girl was home.

She also sent word to Prince Leon that they needed to have a little chat...

He responded with, "we sure do!"

"That's alright, that's o.k. you boys do things your way, and I'll do things mine..." Leon said, straightening his bow tie....

"We'll check ya later, bro!" Braynar said, as they all took off for home...

"Merrill, didn't I just see the boys here?" Raynar asked the wizard.

"Yes, you did, Ray, how can I help you today?"

"Seen my brother today?"

"Not today, I haven't. Why, sup," he asked, voice full of curiosity.

"I haven't heard from Jax.

That's not normal. So, I tried to call Healix and got no response. Was wondering if they'd been by here..."

"No, the only ones by here were 3 royal dragons and royal big kitty... Looking for AlaHanDrea... But, as it turned out, Isabel took her away from Leon...."

They both chuckled at the youngsters drama......

"Well, I'd better go locate my brother's," Raynar told him...

"I can look in my ball, if ya like..." Merrill offered.

"Sure, that would be great, actually. Thanks, man."

"Let's see what we can see..."

"I see Bob! Oh wow, I see Bob in some kind of trouble! Oh no, uh oh..."

"What's wrong, what are seeing?"

"Bobs over by the Cyclopse Peninsula! Those dudes are dangerous, even for Bob!"

"What's he doing over there?"

"Uh oh, it looks like the Cyclopse has visited Tootsies island and made off with some ladies! Bob's gone to get them back!"

"What's that got to do with my brothers?"

"They are watchers, they're watching!" Merrill said, rather sarcastically.

"I wouldn't worry too badly, I also see AlaHanDrea arriving and helping Bob! And, I see Isabel, Cathey Ann and Tootsie!

Uh oh, I see a bunch of lady dragons arriving... Uh, Raynar, you may want to grab George and the boys and head on over there...and take your guards, maybe even your troops!

What I'm seeing hasn't happened yet, but this is the right now future .... You haven't much time!" Merrill warned him...

"How many Cyclopse do you see?"

"More then 100!"

"I'll call the troops! Thanks, Man...."

Raynar headed for the Cyclopse Peninsula, putting out a distress call to the flock.... Queen Isabel is about to be flying into battle at Cyclopse Peninsula! AlaHanDrea and Bob are almost there to engaged in battle!"

The flock dropped what they were doing and headed for the land of the Cyclopse, there least favorite place to be... Dragons were small compared to a Cyclopse!

Thousands of dragons took to the air!

Barbara didn't know what to think. She wasn't feeling well again, so she sat down to enjoy some tea and just wait.

The drones followed the flock, but a few stayed behind to watch Barbara...

———————

"OK, the poles are open:
How many think that Barbara is pregnant?
How many think that Raynar is the father?

How many think the Cyclopse will engage in battle once they see how many dragons they are up against?

Give us your thoughts on the Cyclopse vs Queen AlaHanDrea, King Bob and all of the dragons! Who will prevail?

____

AlaHanDrea sent messages to Bob to wait for her, Cyclopse were extremely dangerous!

He decided to wait...

AlaHanDrea put up a communications screen...

"Greetings Cyclopse community...

I'm Queen AlaHanDrea and this is King Bob.

We've come here for the dragons you took from their island.

We will be needing them back, please."

"Hello Queen Ala whatever Drea..." A big, super bass deep voice boomed.

"You can have your puny dragons... We only got them to make you come here. We want to play with Bob. He looks like fun!"

"You want to play with Bob?"

"Ya, huh uh huh...."

"I don't want anyone hurting Bob!" AlaHanDrea said.

"Us, hurting Bob? I'm more worried about Bob hurting Cyclopse, huhuhhuuh... We just wanna play wit him..."

"What do you think, Bob...

"I think my name is Markus Manus and they should learn it!

By play, do they meet strength contest and stuff?"

"Ya, huhuhhuuh... See those boulders over there? First one to build the wall... Huhuhhuuh...."

"O.k. we do it at the same time or one after the other?"

"Cyclopse go first... Huhuhhuuh ...."

"You've got this, Markus..."

Tootsie said as she arrived.

The dragons all perched to wait and see what was going to happen.

The Cyclopse built his wall in 17 minutes...

Bob built his wall in 13 minutes, 27 seconds.

The next contest was like a pole vault... The Cyclopse got excited when Bob grew himself to their size, then a little bit bigger!"

He managed to jump 7 feet further.......

The next contest was wrestling ..

The rule was, tho, that Bob wasn't allowed to shift out of humanoid ...

They said nothing about the use of magic ... Bob vanished a few times, aggravating the Cyclopse... He finally was able to pin the big brute down, but it took some effort on Bob's part, for sure!

They lifted heavier than heavy objects, did an endurance course, through discs...Bob was able to do everything they could do.

At the end of the last contest, the female dragons were freed.

"We like Bob, uh... Markus... Huhhuuhuhu ....we like him to come battle train wit us... Cyclopse likes Markus Bob! You takes girls back home now, bye bye, you go away now. We see Bob for training! Yes, Markus Bob?"

"Yes. I will love to train with you! Bye now, that was fun!"

Isabel, George and Raynar were relieved that it was simply a contest between giants... Bob shrank himself back down to everyone else's size. "Hey, I kinda like the big boys!" Bob told them.

The flock seemed to really enjoy watching the contests.

The drones really did!

It was humanities first real good look at the Cyclopse community. Gave them a whole new appreciation for how dangerous their planet was...

Chapter 13

"George, have you looked at the latest polls? " Isabel asked him.
"Not really, why?"

"97% say that Barbara's pregnant..."

"What?"

"I'm serious!"

"Well, what would make them say that?"

"George, she's humanoid. Look at her, she's getting big around the middle...

I didn't think you were with her the last couple of months..."

"I haven't been... Raynar?"

"Well, technically, he IS her husband, too! And... You and I have been spending an enormous amount of time together with the new eggs ..." Isabel replied.

"But, a watcher and a humanoid?" George said...

"I dunno. Maybe we should ask the polls...

Hey, you, drone, come over here a minute...

The King and Queen of Taurus 9 would like all y'all's opinions on Barbara .

Who thinks she's pregnant?

Why do you think she is pregnant?

Who do you think the father is and why?

How do you feel about it? Thank you, in advance...

There. Now, let's see what the public has to say."

"Come here drone, I have a different question for all y'all ...

Who is the most beautiful woman in Drakonia?

Who is the sexiest woman in Drakonia?

Who is the most handsome man and who is the sexiest?

Thank you in advance..."

"Oh look George, it's a tie between Me, hmmm that's sweet...

Me, Athena, AlaHanDrea, Barbara, Tootsie, Cathey Ann & Dana!

The triplets are running a close second place! For most beautiful and for sexiest.

They say under sexiest, Mermaids, pick one!" They both had to laugh at that.

Under men, it's between You, Leon, Braynar, Raynar, Jax, Healix, Danalli, Bob, JayDe, Keithen, Kenneth, Craigen, Franklon, Paulio, Thomlin, Brian, Kevin, William, Bjorn and, Carl.

They say that Merrill is in a class of his own...

Peoarin is also in a class of his own.

Carl is in a class of his own...

Kai is in a class of his own.

Leon has an entire category devoted to him!

Braynar also has a Category devoted to him!

The watcher Bros are in their own category....

Oh look... Franklon, Craigen, Kenneth, Paulio and Thomlin are being voted the sexiest of the more mature Dragons... As are you, George!

Danalli seems to have his own category... Ah, he's half human...

Cathey Ann is the most gorgeous of the purple dragons, while Tootsie is the most beautiful of the white dragons! Both as dragons and as humanoid... Impressive!

Oh this is funny...

Mermaids, pick one ...

Athena, hands down!

All mermaids are gorgeous and sexy!

I'm just reading what they are writing!

Queen Isabel has a solo class! None compare to Queen Isabel, a timeless beauty!

Oh, how sweet of so many to say!!! "

"Ya, but look at this poll...

97% believe that Barbara is pregnant and that Raynar is the father! According to the poll, Ray and Barbara had quite a time while you and I were off making eggs ...

97% believe Ray to be the father... Ray sang songs about it to Barbara. The polls say he's known since it happened ... interesting... the polls say that he sang songs to Barbara about it... Sang her songs, Isabel..."

"O.k , well, sounds to me like it's time for a little talk..." Isabel told him.

"Hi there, what's got you two lookin all serious about?" Barbara asked, as she came back in. She froze when she read the polls!

"Pregnant? Me? Wait, what??? I mean, ya, but... Oh wow... Oh wow..."

Raynar, Jax and Healix showed up.

"So, what's up? What's this?" Raynar asked, then read the board...

"It's true, Barbara is pregnant and I am the father. We made a baby, a humanoid watcher... Danalli and Braynar are further tied together with the coming of this child, which, I believe is a girl..."

Everyone began congratulating Ray and Barbara... She was stunned and speechless! She didn't know that she could still make babies!

"Speaking of babies, how many hatchlings are there, George?" Jax asked.

"4.

Girls.

We're trying again."

"Wait, do girls not count?" Barbara asked.

"Well, of course girls count, they are all being raised by the nannies!" George replied.

"All? How many girls do you and George have, Isabel?" Barbara asked.

"Well, now, that's a very good question, Barbara... George, how many girls do we have?" Isabel asked him.

"Girls? Uh, 11, total, I think. 11 or 12.... No, no, I'm sorry, 16. There are 16 girls, total."

"Braynar, Danalli and Keithen have 16 sisters?"

"Ya, they sure do.

We just added 4 more, so now, 20."

"Do watchers count the girls differently?" Barbara asked.

"Oh, well, ya, doesn't everybody?" Jax asked.

"So, it would mean more if my baby is a boy?" She asked.

"No, not mean more... They're different.

Ones not greater than the other.

They are raised how girls are raised and the boys are raised as men are raised .

Girls receive more warrior training and such.

Boys are taught the arts of love n romance... Along with their warrior training.

Boys teach girls by doing....

It's a system that works for us..." Isabel explained

"But I only see you interacting with the boys."

"Girls are more sheltered. More protected... The value of girls is very high, therefore, they are well protected... At least until they are mature ...

Boys are stronger, tougher, more resilient... "

"Oh, I see. So, for baby girl to have been all alone at such a young age... Oh wow! No wonder y'all are all so protective of her! I get it now!"

"Hello, sorry to disturb..." Bob said as he entered the area.

"Hello Marcus Bob, how are you this evening?" Isabel asked him.

"I'm concerned about I'm concerned about Cyclops!" Bob replied.

"As you should be. Cyclops is a very dangerous species... Not just because they are giants, but because they are powerful giants!

They are hoping you're naive enough to fall for their little roos...

They heard about you on the broadcast. Heard how strong and powerful you are.

They want you to play, so they can see what you've got....

So they can learn how to defeat you.

If you train with them, they can learn your weaknesses and use them against you...

They want to test you.

It's best to allow them to believe you can be defeated much easier than reality.

Don't let them see all that you have.

Beat em at their own game and use it to learn about them.

But you must hold back...

Appear less than you actually are...

Much less..."

"I can grow myself to much bigger and be a giant to them..."

"That's great, don't be showing off that skill too much... Not yet..." George added. "Markus, how many Cyclops do you think you can take down at once?"

"Kill or keep alive?"

"Both!"

"Kill, easily a field full of troops. A couple of hundred, no problem.

Keep alive? I dunno, they are kinda strong ... I struggled with the wrestling... Prefer to just make them dead. Is easier, much easier .."

"What if you were faced with an army of 2000? "

"No problem, I can kill them all, very easily."

"Don't let them know that!"

"If AlaHanDrea is together with me, well, we could take out their entire army... Maybe 5 or ten minutes...20 minutes tops..."

"For sure, don't let them know that!" George told him.

"They took the girls to make you go to them... Be careful, man. Those creatures cannot be trusted!" Isabel told him.

"They are going to set traps, make tests... If you don't go to them voluntarily, they will do stuff to make sure you show up! So, don't avoid them. Act eager.... they will target Tootsie, Cathey Ann, even Isabel or one of the boys..." George warned.

"For you, I am Marcus, lovingly known as Bob...

To the Cyclopes, I am Bob... just, Bob..." he said with a smirk, then shifted into Cyclopes! "Think they will like Bob now? "

"Oh! Wow! Bob! You are perfectly handsome, even as a Cyclopes! Look at you!" Tootsie told him, with a big ol smile on her face. "I don't think they are going to know what to think about you, Bob. I just hope they don't decide to kill you. Cyclopes are not very nice!"

"Should they try to kill me, I will destroy every last one of them, their possessions, their homes... I will erase them from the planet! I will kill their friends and their friends friends! Until even their memory lives no more!"

"Easy there now, big guy. Let's not get too carried away... Bob, if they cannot kill you because you are too powerful, they will go after those not so powerful, those you care about... they will find ways to hurt you. I wish they had not become aware of you...."

"I'm considering destroying all of them now and be done with it. Less trouble. I can fix this whole mess and just kill them all right now."

"None of us are going to tell you no. We are also not going to tell you to wipe them out. Just know, that what ever you decide to do about them, we all still love you and support your decision 100%. I will make this suggestion, tho, please get to know them before choosing to remove their species from Taurus 9...."

"o.k, I will stop."

"Bob, you already began to destroy them?"

"Yes, it is the logical thing to do. But, it can wait while I check them out. Thank you all for your counsel. It is appreciated..

I'm stronger than I was before. I like it. I like being part AlaHanDrea! The wizard used her seeds to complete my seeds.... I owe that man my life and my loyalty. I'm conflicted... I'm not supposed to like wizards... I don't like conflict. But, without the wizard, there is no Bob. I'm conflicted. Not good."

"It'll be o.k. Bob. Think of it like this, it wasn't a wizard that saved you... it was Merrill. He just happens to also be a wizard. This is a good example of why I suggested you get to know the Cyclopes before wiping them out.... You may actually like some of them!"

"Ok, you make sense." he said as he shifted back to man state. "Hey, maybe I should let them get to know the real, natural me..." he said, then busted up laughing, making everyone else laugh with him...

Chapter 14

"So, Danalli, your mom's pregnant!
Cool!

And by a watcher, no less! Cool, dude, congrats to the growing family.

So Dude, when are you gonna start reproducing? You've been old enough for quite some time ..." Brian taunted......

Danalli just snorted at him and continued to eat flower blooms off the bush... Trying to ignore him... He got a wicked smile on his face, scooted his rear end in Brian's direction and let one rip! Giggling to himself.... It was a huge one, too!

"Oh man,! Danalli, Dude! C'mon now ... Oh, your disgusting .." Brian said, as he stomped off, snarling over the fresh breath of methane...

"What you giggling... Oh Bro! Was that you?

Oh dude, whatcha been eating?

Dayum!

No wonder your giggling....

Who got it?" Braynar asked, chucking over the ordeal.

"Brian," Danalli answered, still laughing...

They had to leave the area, themselves, just to breath...

"Damn, Bro, being half human, you can really cut some stink bombs!

Way to go!

Brian deserved it!

He'll be smelling that one for a while!" They were both still cracking up over it...

"Maybe he should learn not to poke the dragon," Danalli teased...

"Bro, I don't know about you, but I need some female flesh! Not the baby girl, kind, I mean some seasoned, down and dirty, hot mama, come here big boy, kinda acting, ya feel me?"

"That does sound mighty delicious and I'm awful hungry, bro. Would sound better if she had AlaHanDrea's looks...

body...

And voice..." Danalli admitted.

"Ya, well, dream on, bro...."

"Tell me again why we're in hands off mode... ???"

"My mom said so. Go ahead, go argue with my mother, I dare ya to!" Braynar teased ...

"Na, think I'll pass on that one..."

"Mermaids, dude... Mer... Maids! Feel up to a swim?"

Danalli beat Braynar to the pool!

Just as they arrived and were about to dive in, the water began churning... Much to their delight, it was Athena, herself ..and ... she was in the company of a whole group of mer gals!

The guys wasted not a second shifting back to human state....

"Do you boys feel the need for some seafood?" Athena teased, as she tip toed to kiss Braynar... It was a simple kiss, more of a seductive hello...

"Girls, these fine gentlemen are in the mood for some mood!" Athena told her ladies... And, as luck would have it, just as George was walking up...

"Well, hello ladies! What have we here, sons?"

"Kick off your shoes, pops, it's party time!"

More churning In the pool ... More mermaids! George sent Raynar and Keithen telepathic messages, then decided to invite Merrill, just for giggles and grins...

Poles went up right away! Drummers began drumming, a big fire was lit, mermaids in drylander, climbed up the poles and it was show time!

Nectar barrels were opened... It was time to party!

AlaHanDrea's special, panty dropping nectar, too....

AlaHanDrea heard the ruckus, even tho the party wasn't particularly close. It sounded like fun...but, she was a virgin...again....

Virgins didn't attend those kinds of parties....

Not and remain a virgin...

"Braynar, where's your werewolf?" George asked his son.

"Good question, pops. Braynar summoned him.

His eyes lit up when he say the 'buffet'.... "Hey, thanks, bro!" JayDe told him, with two thumbs up... Then threw his head back and howled!!!!

All of a sudden, a hand was over AlaHanDrea's mouth, strong arms wrapped around her from behind... Successfully pinning her... Kisses on her neck made her knees go week! She didn't recognize the voice, it was in a low whisper. "Don't make a sound, not a peep... Stay quiet. Perfectly quiet... " The strange, deep, male voice instructed.

A blindfold was tied over her eyes, her hands were bound, then strong arms lifted her up and carried her away.

She wasn't sure where she was being taken, or by whom...

The confused and startled teen decided not to struggle too much... Just a little....

Thinking it was just a game...

"Stop your wiggling, now, you be a good little girl.... You are gorgeous, mmmmm mmmm mmm.... The owner of the male voice kissed her on the lips... It was a kiss that shot sparks like nothing she'd ever experienced before! It was incredible!

Heat began rising in her in an instant!

"Just relax, I'm not going to hurt you, I promise you that, virgin.... You are a virgin.... Aren't you?!"

At first, she thought it was Leon, but he didn't kiss like that, his arms didn't feel like the arms she was feeling then... She couldn't figure out who had her...

"My sweet beauty, it's only fair that I tell you, we are not alone right now..."

"You're right, she is magnificent!" A second voice said, as he placed a gag on her. She didn't know whether to be worried or not...

Then she felt her feet being rubbed with some kind of lotion, then her legs...

"Our goal is not to hurt you in any way. Please understand our need for secrecy, your majesty...

You are incredible.....

She wasn't sure she liked them taking her clothes off ... But that didn't stop them... The feel of silk against her skin was reassuring ... The silk was draped across her, lending a bit of exotica to the mix....

But, as good as it felt, she was beginning to get a bit scared.

It was time for this party to end!

Only, she couldn't pop out!

She was trying not to freak out...

Braynar! She screamed in her mind. Braynar! Danalli! Help !!!!!! Keithen!!! Someone, please!!!!! " She couldn't pop out, couldn't use her magic ... She made herself focus as hard as she could and managed to shrink herself enough to get loose and get her blindfold off and gag out of her mouth. She was in a cave!

There were young women hanging in cages, crying and shaking in fear...

A pile of bones, human bones, let her know what was going on.... They were eating those people! Men were grabbing girls out of cages, roughly sexing with them, then they would begin eating the people!

AlaHanDrea had not felt fear quite like she felt it right then!

AlaHanDrea put everything she had into it and managed to shrink herself some more and shifted into a fairy.... It was much easier to hide at 6" tall!

She tucked herself away in some silver moss behind a boulder and continued to cry out for her men....

———————

"Leon, son, what's wrong?" King Leon asked him.

"I thought I heard AlaHanDrea calling out, like she's in trouble! But, faintly...

Wait, there it was again, very faint... Dad, listen...."

"Ya, I hear it, too!

Barely, but I hear it, too!"

"Where's it coming from?"

"Baby girl, summon me and my son!

This is King Leon, summon us at once!"

"Dad, it's not working, let's go look around at her place and see what we can find... There has to be a clue as to where she is,"

The 2 lions tore her place up looking for clues,

for any sign telling them where she might be... They weren't too much worried about making a mess! And they made one hell of a mess!

"King William!" Prince Leon summoned his friend.

"Sup, dudes?"

Need your K9 skills William, we need to locate AlaHanDrea and fast!"

William began sniffing all over the ground, finally picking up a scent. The three took off to go get AlaHanDrea...

William suddenly stopped, tail straight up, ears perked up... "What is it, William?" King Leon asked.

"Gypsum Gypsy's!"

"Are you certain?"

"Absolutely. My pack is on the way..."

"So is the pride!" King Leon said, proudly.

"I notified Bjorn, dad. The bears are already In the air...."

"Good job, son. We're going to need a game plan...

"Dad!

Look!

It's Edward!

The eagles are here!

And look!

Fairies!

Lots and lots of pissed off fairies!"

"Right... On!!!" King Leon said, as he looked out over all of the troops gathering for the rescue effort. They were all stopped in front of him! BJorn and King William stood to his sides...

"Diplomacy is always a good beginning, or, at least an attempt at diplomacy... First, let's sing them a little song, saying hello. On my mark, lions roar, on the next mark, wolves howl! Next, bears! Then the fairies battle cry! Eagles, fly high, screech and watch, screech through the whole thing! ... Lions, Roar!" The sound of an entire pride of giant lions, roaring in unison, was enough to strike fear into All creatures who heard it.

————————

"Wait! Sssshhh! Stop the music!" Braynar yelled.

"Listen! Why are the lions all roaring together like that? The wolves are all howling at one time! What's going on? Dad! The bears! Something's wrong!"

————————

"Wolves!" The unified Howl of the pack was terrifying to hear!

"Bears!" Each species in their turn, as each went off, more showed up, answering the calls of the other wilds...

"All Together now!" Leon called out. "Keep it up for a couple of minutes!!!" Leon ordered...

————————

"You're right, Braynar, I hate to break this party up, but there's trouble in paradise! It sounds like hundreds of creatures, all together! Alert the flock! Let's fly, boys!" George called it. "Hold our spots, ladies, we'll be back!"

George, Braynar, JayDe, Keithen, Danalli and the rest, rushed over to AlaHanDrea's to check on her and found her place a total disaster!

"Dad!" Braynar yelled.

____

King Leon made a hand gesture and it was suddenly quiet.

Too quiet.

Not a creature made a single sound...

The gypsies approached, very cautiously. "Is there a problem your majesties?" They asked the 4 kings that stood before them.

"Yes, there does seem to be an issue requiring settlement. We've come for Queen AlaHanDrea.

We know you have her. Release her at once. I will not repeat myself."

"Now, your majesty, we captured her fair and ......" King Leon was in front of him holding him by his throat before he could finish his sentence.

"Gypsies are about to begin dying, starting with you," he told the gypsy, then bit the man's head off in one quick bite.

"I said, release her at once, are you hard of hearing?"

"Uh, yu, yu, yu, ya, your majejejejesty, uh, wewewee don't seem to know where exactly sshhhhe is at the momomomoment..."

King Leon made the motion for advance and the entire army began marching towards the caves.

The screech and roar of dragons caught everyone's attention just before the sky turned black from the dragons blocking out the sun light...

The gypsies cowered in terror inside of their cave, as King Leon walked in, still dragging the lifeless body of the gypsy he had killed.

He tossed the body inside and let out a planet shattering roar!

AlaHanDrea was never so glad to see her creatures as she was right then!

She ran out from behind the boulder and straight for King Leon! He held out his hand, pulling her into his palm under his own power.

"Are you o.k. baby girl?"

"Yes, and I LoVe you, King Leon! These creatures were going to sex me, then eat me! They are cannibals, too! We can't leave the other girls! I don't mean to deprive a creature of his meal, but King Leon, please, we can't leave them here! They torture!"

"As you wish, my queen."

Release the other creatures, especially the human and humanoids... Do this now or die now!" He ordered, obviously annoyed.

2 more gypsies dropped dead, then another... The creatures were released before any more gypsies were killed... Once all of the creatures were released, the dragons pushed their way in...

George said, "King Leon, Prince Leon, King William, King Bjorn, good to see you again.... AlaHanDrea, glad to see you're in good hands...

My flock is feeling a bit hungry, if y'all don't mind..."

The gypsies began screaming and begging for their lives.

"Certainly, George. Hey, why don't you release the werewolf first, we'd all enjoy watching a bit of his handiwork, we hear he's quite thorough..."

"That, he is. JayDe, you feeling frisky, boy?" George asked him.

JayDe was thrilled! How much different life was for him on Taurus 9! He loved being around those who appreciated his special talents....

King Leon, Prince Leon and the other creature royals, left the cave after witnessing the brutality of JayDe. They decided to take AlaHanDrea home and let the other creatures enjoy that tribe of cannibalistic gypsies.

It was actually quite a large tribe... Before... None remained when the creatures were through!

Over 250 gypsies were in that band... Some of the children and a few women were kept as pets... The rest were mutilated and eaten.

That tribe was no more!

Chapter 15

A few drummers were sitting by the fire, just getting started, when Braynar used his magic to produce a piano, sat down and began a beautiful array of melodies... Keithen showed up, sat down and began playing an instrument similar to a guitar, but it laid on his lap.

Danalli's instrument was almost exactly like a guitar...

The royal brothers sang beautifully together!

"If you can... Believe in you ..if you can't .. then believe in me... I'll hold you up while you hold me ... Together ... We reach our destiny... you and me...

Don't be afraid to look within...don't be afraid to let me in...don't be afraid...... don't be afraid... Have faith in you, have faith in me, have faith in you and me .. like a tree...strong ....with roots so deep... You are the one I want to keep.... I found in you... A hot, burning passion, so fresh, so new...... When you found me .... You found our true destiny... ...don't be afraid.... Let go and let love... ... Heal... ...

What we have together burns hotter than fire, filling us both with burning, yearning, desire.....

let go and let love... ... Heal...

Let... love... heal.......

Don't be afraid.... open your heart ... ...

Let me in.... Let love heal.... Don't be afraid...

(AlaHanDrea chimed in) "oh I'm not afraid... so glad y'all are here... So handsome, so fine, I want to make you mine! I grew up... my eyes can see...just look at you! All y'all have a really nice, uh, gear! Won't you...Follow me... Follow me ... Follow me to my hut... Follow me... Follow me... Follow me... You sure have a nice butt!

Oooh, I wanna squeeze it.. ooooooh, I wanna tease it ... Oooooh, I wanna please it.... Follow me... Follow me.... Oh, won't you follow me to my Hut!

Won't you please follow me... Follow me... Follow me to my hut! I said, follow me... to my hut...... I'm so not afraid! I have no fear.... Follow me to my hut ...."

(Braynar, Keithen and Danalli together), "I will follow you... Follow you... Follow you to your hut... Yes, I will follow you, follow you, follow you to your hut.... But!!!

You're a virgin again!

We're told to touch you is a sin!

Should, we follow you ... Follow you .. follow you to your hut..... Or, should we wait... "

(AlaHanDrea), "maybe... Maybe wait... Maybe y'all all should wait .. want we should have us a debate? To wait or not to wait... the wait... or ....not ...to ....wait... great debate!

I'm not ready for a baby, oooh, baby, ooooh baby! Oh, no no no... No no no no baby.... Maybe y'all should wait ... And keep yo babies to yo self!!!!

If I play with your fanny, I'll end up needing a nanny, please mister, please, keep your babies to yourself! I'm begging, you... oh please, oh please, don't put babies in me....!!!"

Laughter rang out, continuing after the song was through...

AlaHanDrea picked up a microphone... "Braynar, Keithen, Danalli, if you gentlemen don't mind playing a melody for me...

I'd like to dedicate this song to you three, as well as Kenneth, Dane, Leon, and all the rest of you handsome, sexy, yummy..... Well, uh ....

"Okay, so, here's my song....

"When a girl ....grows .... into a woman... .... feelings..... begin to stir... Deep inside... I realize you're sexy, that cannot be denied! I see you as tho it's the first time.... A hunger begins to build... demanding to be filled...

And I want you! I want all of you! .... One at a time...

Well,,, uh.... Well.... Hmmmm ....

ooooops....

Maybe not so much all of you....

Please Mister please, keep your babies to yourself!

Oh,

Please Mister please, keep your babies to yourself!

I look in your eyes and quickly realize

How damned good you would feel...

But I gotta keep it real!

So,

Please Mister, please, keep your babies to yourself!

Your touch makes me tingle all over...

Your kiss makes my knees go weak...

But please please please oh please...

Please hear me when I speak,

Please Mister please, keep your babies to yourself!"

Laughter filled the air, quieted only by the applause, as loud as thunder! Everyone stood, cheering and clapping... Showing how much they agreed with her words and her song.

"Here! Here!" The crowd shouted!

More singers got up to take their turns, continuing on the song that AlaHanDrea had sang... only adding their own verses and their own words... basically saying the same thing that she said. The words, 'please mister please, keep your babies to yourself,' stayed the same, as well as the melody ... Her message was strong.

Fear struck the hearts of the males, as they realized that it would now be more difficult for them to seek pleasure with their females!

As much as the men enjoyed the song at the moment, as the reality of it sank in, they didn't like it so much after all! But, as their luck would have it, that song, and a variety of that song, caught on... and... became the most popular song anyone sang... at least for the women...

As much as the men hated to admit the reason for it, AlaHanDrea's popularity among the men, was lacking after she sang that song... ... and it caught on.

It was difficult for them to not let their feelings show towards her, but she did notice their resentment... And she knew why... she knew exactly why... so, she didn't let it bother her a bit!

Her popularity was never anything she really cared about anyway.

As for the women, they all loved her even more than before! Never having realized they had any control over reproduction........

Chapter 16

"Your majesty, King George, I'm sorry to disturb you, there is a disturbance in the humans technology systems," Brian told his king.

"And that concerns me, Why?"

"Because, they believe that it is an alien interference."

"I see. What about Queen AlaHanDrea's technology, does it also suffer from interference?"

"I wouldn't know, your majesty, I don't have access to it," Brian told him.

King George opened a communications screen and began sending out hello signals, attempting to greet any visitors they might have ..

Much to his amazement, he received a response!

"Greetings Inhabitants of Taurus 9. You received a visitor from our planet. A visitor that you murdered! You murdered him and took his crew hostage, keeping them on your planet with no way to return home!

We are here to free our people! They are our citizens and must be returned to us at once! You may have discovered that there were those afflicted with a condition known as werewolfism, which, is contagious and those effected must be destroyed immediately!

We, are from Beta Centauri. You have one day to return our citizens to us!"

"This is King George, supreme king of Taurus 9. We murdered no one. We defended our planet.

Your citizens crash landed on our planet and remained hidden until they attempted to murder our citizens! We simply defended ourselves!

We also transported a portion of the crew to your world, free of charge.

The portion of the crew that remained on Taurus 9, actually belong here.

Their ancestors were left on beta Centauri by mistake, ions ago.

We simply corrected that mistake!

Beta Centauri persecuted them for being who and what they truly are.

They were liberated from the tyranny they suffered on beta Centauri.

This werewolfism, as you call it, is not a problem here on Taurus 9. As a matter of fact, one of them survived the crash landing. We happen to hold him in high regard! On Taurus 9, he is a king! He lives a good life! We work with his affliction during the times he loses control and utilize his special talents to benefit everyone. Our military loves him!

Why, he even has a seat at the table of the counsel of Kings for our planet!

It's a shame y'all don't know how to properly appreciate the werewolves... No, we will not allow you to destroy King JayDe!" George explained to the aliens ...

"Your words are confusing," the alien commander responded.

"Then allow me to explain things in such a way that you can understand!" George shifted in front of the screen, then shifted back again!

"Does that clear the air for you any?" George asked, rather sarcastically.

"Dragons! I'm speaking with a Dragon??? You're telling me, that we had crew that were, in reality, dragons?

The time of speaking has come to an end! Prepare to be destroyed!" The Alien Commander shouted!

The communication ended.

The planet wide sirens went off! Alerting all citizens to take cover immediately! Evacuate the surface of the planet!

AlaHanDrea looked around for a dragon, but there were none around! Before she sang that stupid song, male dragons were always around! All kinds of male creatures were around... But not anymore! Not since she sang that stupid song and it caught on!

She put up force fields as quickly as she could!

So did the dragons, as well as the rest of the creatures of magic, including Mitchin!

Tootsie showed up.... Cathey Ann and Isabel were there in an instant. Isabel put out a call to all of the female dragons, as well as the dragon riders... All warriors, unite!

AlaHanDrea jumped on Isabel.... They took to the air. AlaHanDrea wrapped herself in Isabel's mane...

A moment later, Isabel was giant sized!

Bob, along with an army of Cyclopse, stood ready on the surface. Bob told the Cyclopse to wait for his signal and quickly flew to join AlaHanDrea and the ladies.

They sensed the launching of a nuclear weapon, with the power to wipe out billions on the surface!

Bob flew over and landed on Tootsie, then rolled himself up in her mane, growing them both to giant size! They joined AlaHanDrea and Isabel, flying towards the bomb at top speed!

Both of them turned their backsides towards the bomb and swatted it with their gigantic tails, sending it flying into the ship that had launched it! Unfortunately, there were more bombs aboard the ship!

They flew as quickly as they could, back towards Taurus 9, trying to avoid the shock waves from the enormous explosion, caused when the bomb struck the alien ship.

Bob shouted at his troops of Cyclops to take cover!

The giant one eyed beasts simply laid on the ground...

Everyone put all they had into powering the shields! Including and especially the cyclops...

Fortunately, the shockwaves didn't reach the surface of Taurus 9! They did, however, slam into the forcefield with enough pressure that they actually caused Taurus 9 to wobble off of its axis! Creating huge quakes,

rock slides and tidal waves, planet wide!

In spite of the catastrophes, the army of Cyclops stood back up, shaking themselves off, cheering for Bob!

They didn't even acknowledge AlaHanDrea or the army of female dragons,

Only Bob!

It seemed they'd follow Bob anywhere! As tho they were his private army! A fact that worried dragon kind, just a bit.

Cyclops possessed strong magic, as well as being giants. Facts that made them a difficult enemy for dragons ... and now they had Bob!

Bob seemed to be developing a love and attachment to the creatures... And them for him ...

Isabel, Cathey Ann and the rest of the all female fleet, were sent tumbling through the air when the shockwaves slammed against the forcefields! It took some doing, but they were finally able to get straightened out enough to land in one piece.

Tootsie still had Bob on her shoulders. She was uncomfortable having to land in the midst of the Cyclops army...

Bob made it clear that Tootsie owned his heart! She was to be treated with respect! If nothing else, treat her with respect out of fear of his anger!!!

Still, she felt nervous to be surrounded by them, so, Bob sent her back to Isabel and the other ladies....

Cheers rose up, as Tootsie approached her own kind!

She stopped in mid air and took a bow before landing ... Causing the ladies to laugh and cheer even louder!

Once she was on the ground, and shifted, she stood between Isabel and AlaHanDrea, took their hands and raised them high in a show of victory!

Of course, the drones were back to broadcasting, so the whole world saw them stand up in a victory stance! And ... even with the quake's, rock slides and flooding from tidal waves, the whole world cheered!

Drones also showed the Cyclops holding Bob up above their heads, carrying him as a show of Victory, and, they whole world cheered even louder!!!

Bob and his troop of Cyclops, were the only males present for the short battle... A fact that George fully intended to address with his male population!

George was well aware of the fact, that the two most important things to all dragons, were sex and food! You just didn't mess with a dragons food or his ability to have sex when he wanted it!

You just didn't!

AlaHanDrea's beauty no longer held the power it once did!

She had a loyalty among the females of most species!

Women looked up to her! Wanted to be like her! If she was going to remain a virgin and refrain from sex to avoid pregnancy, then so were the other females. Even if they were no longer virgins, if they didn't want babies, they were following her lead to not have sex and be exposed to pregnancy.

The male population of most species, quickly grew to resent AlaHanDrea for making it nearly impossible to score sex with their females!

Even married females who didn't want to become pregnant, were refusing sex to their men!

The quake, alone, caused amazing damage in the human sectors of the planet. It effected the creature sectors, just not as badly, since creatures don't build like humans do.

Tidal waves and tsunamis struck planet wide as well! Many lives were lost, but not nearly as many, had the bomb been allowed to strike the planets surface!

Broadcast drones were everywhere, aiding in the search and rescue efforts.

George called for a meeting of all species...

After a lot of deliberation, the creatures decided to assist mankind in their search and rescue efforts, a fact that the broadcast drones were able to notify the humans about.

Humans were usually afraid of big cats, bears, wolves and the like, but, thanks to the broadcast drones, man kind was grateful to the creatures for their help.

The creatures had an incredible sense of smell and hearing and were able to locate the trapped and injured much quicker than human search parties.

It was very unusual for the humans to work with dragons! But at that time, they were extremely grateful for the dragons keen senses, as well as their brute strength, able to move huge boulders and debris the humans would have had to use machinery to move.

Clean up efforts would take some time, but recovery would happen. They were all just thankful that bomb wasn't allowed to strike the planets surface!

The refugees from Beta Centauri, including JayDe, were waiting for George and Isabel when they returned from the human sectors.

"Your majesties, we don't know quite what to say! Please know that we are aware of the sacrifices y'all have made on our behalf and do apologize for what you're having to endure because of us!

Please know how grateful we all are to you.

We deeply regret the lives that were lost, and pray nothing of this nature happens again!" Captain Jackson of the refugees told the king and queen.

JayDe stepped forward...

"I'm forever grateful to you for not turning me over to them! I owe you my life! Tho difficult to do, they would have killed me, for sure. Words cannot express how much I love all y'all, or, how much I love living here, on Taurus 9, with all y'all!"

JayDe bowed down to George, in submission, to show his loyalty and devotion..

"There is another matter I must speak to you about, your majesty. Orphan island has taken amazing damage from the tsunami that all but washed it away. Thank the powers that be that children did not occupy the islands yet.

We will require as much help as we can get to rebuild..."

"Not to worry, King JayDe, your orphan Islands will remain a top priority for rebuilding efforts," George assured him.

The sound of thunder made them all jump...

Great storms were brewing! George was aware that the planet took on damage, but just how much damage, he was not aware!

Ground fog and bright lights announced the arrival of an angel...

It was Sarafina.

"Sarafina! Hello! To what do we owe this honor?" George asked her.

"Taurus 9 has suffered a terrible blow. She has been knocked off of her axis," Sarafina made images appear to explain what she was talking about, showing the planets revolving around their central star.

Then, she showed how the explosion caused the planet to shift slightly, creating a wobble effect. This wobble effect could not be repaired and would forever change Taurus 9.

"George, Taurus 9 will no longer be as she once was! Seasons shall now be suffered. You will experience times of great cold and other times of great heat! There will be times of too much rain, and times of no rain until it seems all will dry up and die, only to have floods occur... Food will no longer be plentiful all of the time.

Famine will occur over portions of the planet. Deserts will be created...

All life is forever changed.

Before the shift, Taurus 9 has been a paradise, I'm afraid that now, she is on a road of death. Her death will not occur in the near future, but occur it will. Until then, all life on her will have to adapt to the new ways.

This is a sad day for Taurus 9. The once beautiful paradise is no more."

"Oh, Sarafina, no! Can we do nothing about this?"

"No, George, there is nothing that can be done to correct it. It is what it is. That explosion was a powerful one! The shields that AlaHanDrea, Bob and the Cyclops population put up prior to the explosion, did an amazing job at protecting the planets surface, unfortunately, when the shockwaves struck them, they did so with enough force that the waves knocked the planet off balance. I'm afraid there is not anything that anyone can do now. It's all just a matter of time.

One more thing before I go. The animal kingdoms have found favor in God's eyes, for their efforts as far as humans are concerned, as well as their efforts among the other animal kingdoms...

Good job! You've proven yourselves more than worthy. When the time comes, you will definitely be relocated.

Please know, during these difficult times, that He is with you!" And with that, Sarafina vanished.

George made a worldwide broadcast about Taurus 9 being off balance and what that was going to mean to everyone on the planet.

His message was played on loop for days on end, while clean up and rescue efforts continued.

AlaHanDrea normally enjoyed storms, but the storms brewing since the planet was knocked off balance, were much too powerful for her. She could only handle taking in a fraction of them.

No one could fully comprehend what was in store for them. They had no concept of winter, or snow... They had no concept of burning hot summers, either.

Life was never going to be as it once was...

Chapter 17

Tens of thousands of females gathered together. Females from all species, all gathered together for the same reason. AlaHanDrea had requested this meeting.

Males, especially male dragons, didn't understand females not wanting to make babies. Making babies was just something that females did! It was nature!

They viewed birth control efforts as a type of murdering the unborn. They saw ways of preventing pregnancy, as a way of killing them, before being created.

To prevent their creation was unforgivable to many creatures, especially dragons!

Reproducing was the natural thing to do! Preventing it was just wrong, as far as they were concerned.

The women refusing sex and the planet being knocked off balance, was creating a hellish environment for everyone! It was way too much change, way too quickly.

"Greetings Ladies!" AlaHanDrea began, standing on a tall stage, for all to see.

Broadcast drones from all over the planet, hovered above.

"Welcome to the Conference of ladies!

We are women!

Hear us roar!" Applause rang out louder than thunder.

"I come to you today to discuss the subject of reproduction.

When I sang that song, I had no idea the impact it was going to have.

Ladies, please understand that I never meant to make anyone think I'm against reproducing!

Quite the contrary!

Reproducing is a beautiful thing!

Please try to understand, things are different for me.

For one thing, my life span is greater than most ever dreamed of.

Barring any accidents, I should live for thousands of years!

I have more than plenty of time for reproduction!

In addition, there is not another of my species.

I am the only one like me.

I do not even know for sure that I Can reproduce!

Also, I'm more than a creature, I am also a weapon!

The best weapon Taurus 9 has against alien intrusions.

Well, Bob and I are.

As a weapon, I have a responsibility to the planet, as well as it's population.

Had I been pregnant when that bomb was launched, I could not have helped to save the planet from destruction!

I'm not against reproduction at all!

As a matter of fact, I have decided that now is as good a time as any, for attempting to reproduce!

If a suitable male does not volunteer, I have been assured medical assistance in becoming pregnant or laying eggs, which ever I can successfully do.

I apologize from my heart for leading you to think that reproduction was anything other than something to be celebrated!

If you're married, please go home and make your man glad he's a man! If your not married, but are sexually active, pick a partner and celebrate being alive!

Just please, before making a baby, please make sure your able to care for the infant, that's all I ask.

Please forgive me for leading you down the wrong path!

It was never my intention!

Thank you for hearing me!"

When AlaHanDrea turned to leave the stage, Leon was standing there, ready to escort her to anywhere she wanted to go!

With the whole world watching, he pulled her close and kissed her with love and passion!

The applause were louder than thunder!

Leon scooped her up in his strong arms and carried her off stage, with women hollering and applauding like nothing they had ever heard before!

Queen Isabel took the stage. "Ladies, may I have your attention please!

Well, it appears that Queen AlaHanDrea had a volunteer!

Yes, good for her!

And What a volunteer, I might add!

Did you ladies get a good look at Prince Leon?

Is he hot or what?

Of course, Prince Leon is a giant, flying Lion.

Should she reproduce with him, she's liable to get a litter!"

Laughter rang out so loud, no one could even hear themselves think.

"Ladies, I'd like to introduce to you, Princess Athena and her band of Mermaids!"

"Hello, ladies! I'd like to speak to you about the power of being female!"

The cheers were deafening...

"I don't know about all y'all, but I like being a woman!" She said, pushing her breasts up with her hands!

"I like being a woman!

I love teasing and pleasing men!

I love it when men can't get enough of me, don't you?

Being sensual is fun, ladies!

Being seductive is fun!

It's exhilarating!

Being wanted is fulfilling!

We owe it to our men, as well as to ourselves, to be as sexy, sweet, seductive and sensual as we can possibly be!

If you want your man to be happy, make him happy!!!

These beautiful ladies have volunteered to show all y'all what pole dancing is!

Both men and women are a fan of pole dancing!

Ladies, the art of arousal can be learned!

Give that man a hard on, and he will follow you into your bed!

Make him feel like the man he is!

Enjoy him and make sure he knows that you enjoy him!

Let him know that you hunger for him!

Let him know that you desire him!

Please, enjoy the show!" More cheers and applause as the mermaids climbed the poles to show off their incredible skills...

Once the show was over, the meeting was dismissed.

Woman rushed to get home, back to their men.

Ground fires were lit... Barrels of nectar were placed about, in anticipation of the women... Special nectar! Yes nectar!

The creatures, as well as humans, of Taurus 9, probably had more sex happening on that night than ever in their history!

"I've waited for this since you were a bitty baby!" Leon said to AlaHanDrea as he laid her down in the bed. There wasn't much else in that hut, besides a bed.

"Oh Leon! I do love you! But Leon, I'm scared!"

"Don't be scared sweet woman, I'm not going to hurt you... I'm going to make you feel a lot of things, but pain isn't on the list!" He told her, then kissed her passionately, lighting a fire deep inside.

"Trust me and relax!" He told her, as he gently bound her wrists together. She could free herself quite easily, should she want to.

He placed a blindfold loosely over her eyes, more for sensory deprivation... He wanted her focussed on what she was feeling.

By the time it was time to do the deed, she was beyond ready for him!

He took his time at first, but soon, they were both caught up in the passion!

"Oh Leon! Leon! Wow! That was beyond incredible!"

"Thank you. I thought so, too. Medical assistance... Very funny... As if ..."

"I take it you approved of my speech?"

"Yes. When mother told me that you called for a meeting of the female population, I rushed right over. I thought you might need protecting... I was very relieved when I heard what you had to say! You redeemed yourself today. Hear those drums? Parties are breaking out all over the planet! Men everywhere are having sex tonight, thanks to you! Good job! This whole planet was getting difficult to handle!"

"I never meant for the women to cut their men off."

"Maybe not, but 'please mister please, keep your babies to yourself' put a halt to sex, planet wide!

There's nothing worse than a bunch of unfulfilled, horny males!! The only thing worse would be Hungry, unfulfilled horny males!

AlaHanDrea, I've been meaning to ask you a question. Why did you not bite the gypsies?"

"I would have, had they gotten ahold of me again. When I was blindfolded, I didn't know who they were or what they wanted. My venom is certain, instant death.

I do not enjoy killing. I really don't."

"Did you enjoy being rescued?"

"I'm grateful to have been rescued."

"But, did you enjoy the act of being rescued?"

"I'm not sure enjoyed is the correct emotion. Their was nothing enjoyable about the entire event.

I felt, grateful, embarrassed, humbled, embarrassed, weak, um, loved, supported, adored, scared, apprehensive, worried... Enjoyed? No, not on the list...

Why would you think I enjoyed it?"

"AlaHanDrea, you are a very powerful creature. I've personally seen you take out an army of aliens at 7 years old... I'm trying to figure out how it is that you needed rescued from a band of gypsy's."

"For one, I didn't know who they were at first. Second, my magic wasn't working in that cave...I was honestly scared. Yes, I was prepared to bite, but, I only have a certain amount of venom!

I don't reproduce venom fast enough, and without my powers, I felt so...... vulnerable........."

"I'm so sorry, baby, I was wrong...I should have known better than to think the way I was thinking... I feel terrible... How could I think that way about you? I'm glad that we were able to be there for you, baby. I honestly am."

"You thought I enjoyed being rescued? That I called for help because I enjoyed being rescued???"

"I'm ashamed of myself. Boy, am I ashamed of myself."

"Don't be. I can see how you could think that, I mean, with your juices all backed up, like they were, and all ..." She teased.

"Oh, ha ha..."

"So, Leon, when you showed up at the meeting, you had no idea what I was going to say? You came there thinking you might need to save me?"

"Well, ya...but then, I heard your message and got a rock hard boner," he teased....

"Leon, thank you for being there! You rock! No one else showed up, just you! Ya, I'm glad that you were first! I'm real glad that you're first...."

"Ya, me too! Can I be second, too? He teased, then laid her on her back and kissed her with passion... again...

Chapter 18

The party with the mermaids left Braynar, Keithen, George, Kenneth, Craigen, Franklon, Mitchin and Paulio very hung over!

They could barely move when they began waking up. One at a time, they'd crawl over and flop over into the pool... Sink, and sit on the bottom, in dragon state, of course...well, except for the vacationing angel...

AlaHanDrea, Isabel, Tootsie, Cathey Ann and Athena all swam over to pester and tease the hung over men...

They couldn't help themselves...

AlaHanDrea noticed that Danalli wasn't among them...quietly slipping away, back up to the surface, to look for him.

She couldn't find him among the fall out from the party, so, she took a chance and went to his lair.

Young ladies weren't really supposed to go into a male dragons lair unescorted ...

But, she threw caution to the wind and went in to look...

Sure enough, he was home. From the looks of things, he'd stayed home all night...

AlaHanDrea used her magic to produce two mugs of chocolate coffee.

"AlaHanDrea, I didn't hear you come in!"

"I thought you might like a mug of coffee."

"Thank you," he said, then took the mugs from her, sat them on the end table, took her in his arms and kissed her a kiss that made Sparks fly!

She melted in his arms!

Danalli picked her up and carried her over to his lounge by the fireplace and laid her down. He snapped his fingers and their coffee was on the end table by them, then he kissed her again, filling her with burning desire!

Danalli was in no one's hurry. He'd waited a very long time to make her his... This time, it was really her... She wasn't dying... She was all grown up and there was not a reason one why he couldn't finally have what he'd longed for since she was a young girl.

He knew she was going to be amazing as a woman and he wasn't wrong!

"Oh Danalli, baby, you take my breath away!

Danalli, what's wrong, baby, are you o.k?" She asked, full of concern.

All of a sudden, he was showing signs of shifting back to dragon, as if he was having a difficult time remaining in Human state.

"Ya, I"ll be o.k. Just let me shift for a little bit..." He said, a moment later, he was all dragon.

AlaHanDrea got up, went over to him and began softly kissing all over his face, while stroking his face and his mane, talking softly to him.

"You are such a magnificent Dragon! I appreciate you and love you in man state, but I believe I love you even more as a dragon!

The only problem is, I can't actually make love to you in dragon state... and that's a problem, because I really, really want to make love to you!"

He shifted back in an instant, when she said that! Took her in his arms and kissed her with a hot passion that set her on fire! He was much more aggressive than before!!

He tore her clothes off of her....

Several hours later, as they were laying, breathless on the lounge, he rolled over, looked deeply into her eyes, then kissed her with a loving passion... Then made gentle love to her, that escalated as the passion built.... Gone was the aggressive hunger... The loving passion was also incredible!

Danalli felt it when it happened!

"AlaHanDrea, we did it baby!"

"Did what?"

"You and I made an egg! Yes ma'am, we just made an egg! It won't be long before you lay that egg and I will carry it in my pouch...... Oh, uh oh... wow! Oh wow! Oh, cool! We're going to be parents!" He kissed her again, then laid with her in his arms, smiling...

"We made a baby, Danalli?

You and I made a baby?

Really?

We're really going to be parents?

Well, ya!

Hey...

How do you guys always know?"

"We can feel it happen. We can feel the spark the creating of life makes."

"Nice. Very nice... How long does it take for me to make an egg?"

"Sweetie, has no one ever explained all of this to you?"

"No, not really."

"Baby girl, your body makes eggs every day. If those eggs fail to come into contact with the male sperms, your body absorbs them. However, when a male sperm catches an egg and manages to penetrate the shell, then the egg is fertilized, creating life. Then, about a day or so later, you lay the egg.

If no male is present, either you, or a stand in, must sit on the egg, or eggs, to keep them warm. If a male is present, he puts the egg, or eggs, in his protective pouch, keeping it, them, safe and warm. Until it, they hatch."

"I make eggs every day?

So, if I have sex everyday, it's possible that I could reproduce a baby a day or, possibly even more? And if I do it with different males the children will all have different dad's?"

"Well, ya. Sex makes babies. Not every single time, but ya, sex makes babies ... It's how the world is populated."

"Danalli, do it to me again and make another baby. I want another one with you, right now... Please?"

"Woman, you do not have to ask me twice!" He said, then kissed her with so much love and passion, she was totally lost in that kiss!

"AlaHanDrea, baby girl, we made twins!"

"We did? We made 2 more? Cool! I'm so excited!

Will I lay them all at once?

Does it hurt???"

"It's a bit uncomfortable. I'm not sure, at the same time, but probably on the same day... tomorrow, they should come out..."

"What do I do until the eggs come out?"

"You should probably get some rest, truthfully."

"Danalli, is George carrying eggs in his pouch?"

"Yes, he has a whole pouch full!

Its only fair to tell you, not all eggs are successful. Please don't get upset if some of them fail. If they do, we will just try again!"

"Oh, o.k. Im going to have dragon babies! You and I, we, are going to have dragon babies! Well, dragon and a whole bunch of other stuff all mixed up! I'm sleepy..." A moment later, she was fast asleep.

"Well, I guess you were sleepy!" Danalli said out loud to no one in particular. He held her close and drifted off to sleep with her in his arms, her head laying on his chest...

Danalli woke up first. She hadn't moved since she fell asleep! He decided to lay there for a few minutes before waking her up.

He didn't have long to wait! Cramping woke her up. She jumped up out of bed and hurried to a place of privacy where she could relieve herself.

"Danalli! Danalli! Come quick!" she yelled.

Danalli! Eggs! Our eggs!! Hurry!"

He jumped up, rushing in to see for himself...

3 eggs laid in the soft grass. 2 of them were the spotted eggs of boys! Danalli was so proud of them!

2 boys!

He carefully scooped them up, tucking them safely away in his pouch.

"Danalli, you're pregnant! You are growing babies in your belly pouch, you are pregnant! "

"Yes, I suppose I am! Let's see how long it takes anyone to notice, before we make the announcement...."

"Great idea...." She agreed...

"Danalli! Are you home? Danalli?" George called out.

"Yes, I'm home, I'm down here, come on in...."

AlaHanDrea vanished when she heard George...

"Danalli.... Something's different.... Uh! You've reproduced! You have eggs!

Oh, let grandpa see!" George insisted.

"Well, would you look at that!

2 boys and a girl!

Way to go, son!

Way to go! Who's the mother? Dare I ask..."

The look on Danalli's face said it all!

"Way... To... Go... Son!!!"

Chapter 19

"Shhhh, everybody, ssshhhhh, be quiet! Listen!" Braynar commanded everyone around the campfire...

When Prince Braynar shhhhh-ed people, they got quiet!

The faint sound of beautiful flute music was in the breeze. The sound was getting louder, indicating the players were getting closer. The drummers began softly drumming to the beat of the flutes, just loud enough for the players to hear, as if to say, please come join us... Which, they did...

4 very lovely young ladies come walking up the path, playing their flutes...

No one had seen these girls before, leading the group to believe they were with the new refugees... They weren't wrong...

One at a time, the young ladies shifted, then shifted back, saying their names...

"Hi, I'm Emilie."

"Hi, I'm Amelia."

"Hi, I'm Amy!"

"Hi! I'm Mellie Mae!"

"We're the Bonner sisters," they said in Unison, then went back to playing their flutes.

Applause rang out, welcoming the girls to the group.

The girls up stepped the tempo of the music ...

Braynar made his piano appear, Keithen sat down with his xyclon, (a lap guitar looking instrument), and it was on!

Danalli heard the music, grabbed his sitar and hurried over to the fire.

Kenneth and Brian hurried over when they heard the dance beat...

Both of them grabbed microphones and began singing.

A couple of more refugee ladies wandered over to the group and began dancing to the music.

It wasn't long before a full blown party broke out!

It was just what everyone needed, too... it was only the second party to happen since the ladies had cut off sex for a bit.

Danalli felt kind of strange, quietly got up and excused himself...

"Listen, George, it's a party! I'm so glad to hear that! Maybe things can begin to get somewhat back to normal," Isabel said.

"I dunno, I'm disturbed by what the Angel said. I wonder, if I had handled things differently, if maybe that alien wouldn't have tried to destroy the planet with that nuclear bomb."

"George, he came here looking for a fight! He even said so when you first began the conversation. My question is, what was he doing, flying around the cosmos with a nuclear bomb aboard his vessel?"

"That's actually a very good question, sweetheart. Maybe we should present that question to your other husband ... Speaking of which, where is Raynar?"

"I actually haven't seen him or his brothers since before the alien .." Isabel commented.

"That's weird. You'd think they'd have been all over this situation ... Have you spoken to Merrill?" George asked with a bit of concern in his voice.

"No, haven't you? And, where's Barbara?" Isabel asked.

"Maybe Barbara is with Raynar...? I think we need to summon them.

Isabel, have you seen AlaHanDrea?"

"Come to think of it, no, I haven't seen her, either. Instead of summoning them, we should go to where ever they are, don't you think?" Isabel asked.

"I dunno Izzy, we might not like the outcome of that. I like the idea of summoning better." George told her.

"Dad! Mom! Isabel! Mom! Dad! Isabel! Oh, Isabel... DAD!" Danalli called out, as he ran towards them, obviously in distress...

"Danalli, what's wrong? It's the eggs, isn't it? What's wrong with the eggs?" George asked.

"Eggs? What eggs? No one told me about any eggs!" Isabel exclaimed.

"The girl egg absorbed the other two!!! Dad! The boys are gone!"

"What? Oh no! Oh no!" George said.

"Eggs? What eggs? Danalli, I didn't know your were expecting... Why didn't y'all tell me? What do you mean, they are gone?"

"I'm sorry Isabel, I wasn't telling anyone yet. I had 3 eggs! 2 boys and a girl! The boys are gone! The boys are gone, dad! The boys are gone!"

"Calm down, Danalli, you're not doing yourself any good getting so upset. I know, I know, this situation is extremely upsetting, just, please, try to calm down..." George told him.

Danalli removed the egg from his pouch and carefully laid it in on a pile of soft moss.

There was movement inside the egg. A lot of movement.

"It's early for the eggs to even try to hatch. Way too early. What's going on here, dad?"

"HEALIX!" George called out.

"Yes, George, what's going on. Are your eggs about to hatch?" Healix asked.

"No, that's Danalli's egg."

"Oh, I didn't know you were expecting."

"No one did, Healix, there were 3 eggs, 2 boys and a girl, but the boys are gone! I think the girl absorbed them!"

"Why, is AlaHanDrea ... Ah, she is, isn't she? Here, let me check this out... Danalli, jump up on the table and let me check you out a minute...

Now, just sit back and relax, I'm just going to feel around for a moment...

Ah, here it is... 1 egg, 2 eggs!"

"What? Where'd you find them? Oh, what a relief!"

"They migrated away from the baby powerhouse their sister seems to be. Shall we take a look inside and see what's going on?"

Before anyone could answer one way or another, Healix had a viewing screen up, touched the female egg and images showed of the baby inside.

"She looks like a dragon to me!" George said.

"AlaHanDrea is the mother? Way to go Danalli! Looks like a dragon to me, too!" Isabel told him.

Danalli just sat there, with a stunned look on his face. That's my daughter! My baby girl!" Danalli picked her up and gently placed her back inside of his pouch. One of the boys looked like a human embryo!

"Don't look so shocked, Danalli, you're half human and AlaHanDrea has some human in her make up as well. It's strange seeing a human embryo inside of a dragons egg, but hey, it looks to be healthy enough." Healix told him.

"Wow! I have 3 babies!" Danalli said, feeling kind of dazed. "Where's my mom?"

"She's with Raynar and Jax. They are over watching AlaHanDrea help some Islanders with a problem they've been having.

It's take your baby mama to work day..." Healix said with a chuckle.

"Where were y'all when the alien attacked?" Isabel asked.

"Watching, it's what we do..." Healix joked. " We were watching. Then, we helped put up the forcefield... That was a nuclear bomb!"

"Well, thank you!" Isabel told him.

"There was no good answer, Izzy, no matter what we did, massive damage was eminent. There was just no way to avoid damage. Poor Taurus 9, we tried to protect her, we honestly did. She could have healed her surface, eventually, maybe, but this damage cannot be reversed ... "

"But Healix, what about y'all in your natural state? Can you not fix it then?" George asked.

If I touch her, even lightly, it will kill everyone and everything on her surface. Life is such a delicate balance.

Taurus 9 fits in the palm of my hand! Attempting to rebalance her, would destroy her," Healix explained. Then, he went over to a tree, plucked a small plum and set it in his hand. He placed it between two fingers as tho he were going to pick it up. "See how much of the surface just my fingers cover?"

"Well, what about God?" George asked.

"God weeps for Taurus 9! She is one of His beloved. God is a creator.

The creator.

He creates, he does not sit around running things. He creates, then nature takes it's natural course. He does not interfere with freedom of choice.

All creatures are free to live their lives as best they can.

Those who live their lives right, bring joy to His heart. Those that don't, put tears in His heart.

He weeps when his children die too soon.

He weeps when His children suffer.

What happened to Taurus 9 broke His heart.

Still, it was the result of man's free will choices.

Situations such as this, are where we come in. We relocate worthy life forms when the time comes for Taurus 9 to end.

She still has a great number of years left before that happens... Hard years, life here will not ever be the same.

"So, no intervention?" Isabel asked.

"No. No intervention. It is what it is. I'm sorry."

"We're going to need shelters, aren't we?" Isabel asked.

Actually, dragon kind and other cave dwellers will be fine. The temperature inside of caves stays the same, no matter what. But, you will need to stockpile food of all kinds ... either that, or learn to hibernate...

Volcanic activity is going to increase, please pick your mountains with that in mind."

"I'm going to be a daddy," Danalli said, smiling, changing the subject...

"Yes, you are!" Isabel said, laughing at how he just shut the other men up...

Chapter 20

Everything on the island seemed calm enough, for the moment.

The chief and the medicine man were telling AlaHanDrea stories of the monster from the sea.

AlaHanDrea loved the innocence of the islander's who lived on the strip of islands, so far out in the middle of the sea, unspoiled by technology.

The human population knew the islands were there, they just left them alone, out of respect.

Taurus 9 was an enormous planet, with no shortage of land. There was no need to disturb those islander's.

According to the chief, the monster was a gigantic water dragon, with a really bad temper!

She suddenly appeared just over 30 years ago and has grown considerably!

He summoned AlaHanDrea on the advise of islander's visiting from other regions...

As a thank you to AlaHanDrea for showing up, a luau was planned for that night.

The chief was blown away by AlaHanDrea's rare beauty.

According to the medicine man, one could tell that she was deadly dangerous, because anything that beautiful had to have thorns to protect itself...

The Chief had always been of the opinion that the deadlier the poison, the more beautiful the flower...

Tall poles lined the beach. Pigs were being roasted over open fires near the waters edge.

Long tables full of fruits, vegetables, nuts and the like, set parallel to the poles, further away from the waters edge.

The drummers drummed and young ladies did the hula type dance...

Young warriors came out dancing with wands, lit on fire on both ends... It was really something to see!

Warriors began running up those poles, then began some incredible acrobatics from high up near their tops...

AlaHanDrea wondered how the islander's would react if they saw how the mermaids used those poles!

Suddenly, the ocean began to churn!

The warriors on the poles hurried down, screaming about the monster coming out of the sea!

The warriors grabbed their spears, making ready to attack!

Islander's fled the beach in fear of the monster...

The islander's description of the monster was actually pretty accurate, she did resemble a dragon!

AlaHanDrea told the islander's to relax and flew out to see the monster.

When she got close, she said, "hello there, my name is Queen AlaHanDrea, what's your name?"

"Millie. My name is Millie. You can understand me?" The monster asked.

"Yes, I sure can. I can also breath under water. Let's go under and have a chat, O.K?"

"Sure, O.K." Millie agreed.

"You certainly are a beautiful girl!

So Millie, why all of the trouble with the islander's?"

"Thank you! I don't know what their problems are, they are a bunch of unfriendly, mean hearted, rude... I try to go up and introduce myself, and they throw spears at me!" She explained.

"Oh, ya, they are afraid of you.

Can you shift?

Can you make yourself look like a human?"

"Huh? Make myself look like a human?"

"Sure! I'll bet you can do it. Just concentrate real hard on looking like a human, think about it really hard!" AlaHanDrea instructed.

Just as she suspected, Millie could shift!

"Well, would you look at me!" Millie exclaimed.

"AlaHanDrea! Hey! I heard you were over here!" Athena Called out. "I see you've met my good friend, Millie. And Millie, you look beautiful! I didn't know you could do that!" Athena told her.

"Oh, you two know each other?" Millie asked.

"Ya, Athena has been my best friend ever since I was born!

She took care of me as a baby, because my mommy was dead.

Dane became my boyfriend before I could even walk!"

"Well, that's wonderful! Are we going to be friends as well?" Millie asked, her voice sounding hopeful.

"I thought we already are!" AlaHanDrea told her. Millie just smiled.

"Millie, what inspires you to go up and introduce yourself to the humans?" AlaHanDrea asked her.

"Parties. They throw parties and I wanna go!

I get so bored!

And it looks like so much fun!

But I'm never invited," she said with a frown.

"Tell ya what, let's you and I go up and I will introduce you to the natives in your human form.

Let it look as tho I'm rescuing you...

Athena, why don't you go grab some merfolks, it's time to meet the locals!"

"You got it, baby girl!

See ya in a few!" Athena said, then swam off in a hurry.

"Come on Millie, take my hand, we're swimming to the surface, oh wait, here, let me put some clothes on you....

There, that's better. I want you look as tho you've been captured a bit..." She explained.

The dress was more like a mid thigh length tank top, kind of tattered. AlaHanDrea placed a princess crown on her and headed for the surface. They both looked as tho they bobbed to the surface, then, Millie put her arms around AlaHanDrea's neck and was flown to the beach.

Islander's came running to see the girl from the ocean. "The creature won't be bothering you anymore!" AlaHanDrea told the chief.

"Oh! That's wonderful news! A thousand thank you's!!!

You found this girl under the sea?" The chief asked, astounded at her presence.

"Yes, I went under to see about the monster, and there she was! Trapped... So, I freed her and brought her up to meet y'all. She doesn't remember much of her life. She's alone in the world..." AlaHanDrea explained...

"Hi, I'm Millie," she said to the chief.

"Welcome Millie, we're glad to have you here with us! You are really quite beautiful!

But, how did you not drown?

Here, my daughter's will take you and get you settled, find you some clothes and fix your hair. My men will make you a hut of your own.

Once you get fixed up, please, come join the party," the chief told her.

"Oh, thank you so much!" Millie said, then went off with the other ladies.

"Chief, Millie is an amphibian... she isn't exactly human...

Now, as you know, I'm not from Taurus 9, tho, I've been here since I was just 6 years old.

I brought some friends with me from Ion 6.

They are actually your neighbors..."

"Our neighbors, I'm afraid I don't understand..."

"They breath in water chief, they live under the sea. I invited them to come up to the surface, meet y'all and get aquatinted. Princess Athena is bringing a group with her.

They are called Mers. Mermaids are women and of course, MerMen....

They have the ability to change their tail fins for legs, in order to be on dry land.

I think you will love them. See the churning in the water? The people of the sea are about to surface!"

The chief was speechless! Everyone was! They were in Awe of the people walking up from out of the sea!

"I had no idea that there were people living in the sea! Or that beautiful women were amphibians!

Wow!

Such beautiful people!" The chief exclaimed!

"Hello, chief, I'm Princess Athena, daughter of King Neptune, God of the seas, and these are my people. Nice to finally meet our neighbors!"

"Very nice to meet you, Princess Athena." The chief said, kissing her hand.

The drummers resumed drumming and the party restarted.

Mermaids love a good party! The girls climbed right up those poles and showed off their considerable skills.

The islander's were amazed at the body control and strength the mers possessed... Both male and female...

Some of the mers decided to show of their acrobatic roller dancing skills, they had been taught by the triplets and their husbands.

The locals were really enjoying being entertained by the neighbors they never knew they had...

The medicine man approached the chief, "Did I hear Princess Athena Correctly? Her father is the God of the Seas?"

"I believe you did!"

"That makes her a Goddess, as well as a princess... Interesting......"

The ladies on the poles all stopped dancing, turned towards the open Sea, then became very excited... King Neptune was coming up in his full intimidating self... Parade and all...

"Chief! It seems my father has arrived!" Athena announced, like a good daughter.

Since King Neptune was being carried, he remained in Mer State, so the locals could get a good look at him, then he shifted to man state... Putting his drylander on...

After the introductions were made, King Neptune invited the chief and medicine man, as well as any islander's interested, to go down under the sea in the tunnels and get a good look at the life of the mer folks...

The chief got very excited about the Kings Resort.

"Your majesty, you must be as excited as I am about Queen AlaHanDrea killing the sea monster," the chief asked King Neptune.

AlaHanDrea butted in, "Oh, No, I didn't kill the sea monster.

There was no reason to.

We had a chat and she promised not to scare y'all any more.

She wants y'all to promise not to throw spears at her, just because she's different.

You see, she gets lonely, and when y'all throw parties, she wants to go, but y'all always attack her, trying to kill her, so, she runs back into the sea.. usually crying her eyes out, heart broken and rejected..

Ya see, if she wanted you dead, you'd be dead.

She is quite the capable creature!

Her magic is powerful!

She doesn't want to hurt y'all, so, she just goes back into the sea. AlaHanDrea explained.

"You're hating on her out of fear, because of how she looks, without ever getting to know her.

Yet, based on looks, you took in Millie over there, gave her a home, clothed her, fed her, offered her friendship, without ever realizing that she could destroy this island with very little effort on her part, had she a mind to."

The look on people's faces was priceless ...

"What you say is true. We judged by appearances, but, please, what do you mean, Millie could destroy this island?" The chief asked.

"Chief, Millie IS the sea creature! She has the power to shift. She didn't know that she could before I showed her how...

She is a lovely being that has the power to protect you from all of your enemies! She loves very deeply and is very protective over the ones she loves!" AlaHanDrea told the chief.

"Millie, come here a moment please. Millie, please breath fire at the ocean.

"Well, o.k. but, everyone has been so nice to me, I don't want to ruin things here, AlaHanDrea."

"They are going to find out sooner or later, Millie, it's just going to have to be o.k "

"Well, OK, if you say so."

Reluctantly, Millie did as instructed.

Stunned silence ....

Then, slowly, applause rose up from the islander's!

Millie looked out over the crowd and took a bow ...

Everyone cheered for her. Tears rolled down her face.... Tears of joy... For having been accepted as is ... They were loving her just as she was!

There was no greater feeling than being accepted as is!

As if testing them, Millie shifted back to normal, roared very loudly, then blew fire at the sky!

She very quickly shifted back to human form...

The applause and cheers were deafening!

Don't miss out!

Visit the website below and you can sign up to receive emails whenever Jeri Andrew publishes a new book. There's no charge and no obligation.

https://books2read.com/r/B-A-YGIAB-MDIQC

BOOKS 2 READ

Connecting independent readers to independent writers.

About the Author

Retired, I now spend my time writing stories from my imagination, to share with others, to help carry them away to another world, a world of magic and intrigue...